"Looks like we're in for a wicked night."

Startled, Shelby spun around to see Rafe standing in her doorway.

Lightning flashed. Without warning, Rafe lifted her into his arms.

"Put me down!"

"Hush, green eyes," he murmured. "I'm taking you to safety."

Shelby was pulled against his solid chest, her hands gripping his muscular arms. His strength and the sound of his voice soothed her.

But she knew she couldn't continue leaning on him. She wanted a home, a husband, children...but experience had taught her that the only person she could depend on was herself. She pushed against his massive chest, trying to break his hold, but his grip tightened.

She melted against him. Maybe she *could* linger in Rafe's arms, for just a little longer....

* * *

WITH THESE RINGS

The Secret Millionaire (SE #1252)
Her Surprise Family (SR #1394)
The Man, The Ring, the Wedding (SR #1412)

Dear Reader,

September's stellar selections beautifully exemplify Silhouette Romance's commitment to publish strong, emotional love stories that touch every woman's heart. In *The Baby Bond*, Lilian Darcy pens the poignant tale of a surrogate mom who discovers the father knew nothing of his impending daddyhood! His demand: a marriage of convenience to protect their BUNDLES OF JOY....

Carol Grace pairs a sheik with his plain-Jane secretary in a marriage meant to satisfy family requirements. But the oil tycoon's shocked to learn that being *Married to the Sheik* is his VIRGIN BRIDE's secret desire.... FOR THE CHILDREN, Diana Whitney's miniseries that launched in Special Edition in August 1999—and returns to that series in October 1999—crosses into Silhouette Romance with *A Dad of His Own*, the touching story of a man, mistaken for a boy's father, who ultimately realizes that mother and child are exactly what he needs.

Laura Anthony explores the lighter side of love in *The Twenty-Four-Hour Groom*, in which a pretend marriage between a lawman and his neighbor kindles some very real feelings. WITH THESE RINGS, Patricia Thayer's Special Edition/Romance cross-line miniseries, moves into Romance with *Her Surprise Family*, with a woman who longs for a husband and home and unexpectedly finds both. And in *A Man Worth Marrying*, beloved author Phyllis Halldorson shows the touching romance between a virginal schoolteacher and a much older single dad.

Treasure this month's offerings—and keep coming back to Romance for more compelling love stories!

Enjoy,

Mary-Theresa Hussey

Mary-Theresa Hussey
Senior Editor

HER SURPRISE FAMILY

Patricia Thayer

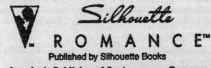

Silhouette
ROMANCE™
Published by Silhouette Books
America's Publisher of Contemporary Romance

To the special guys in my life, Jeff, Brett and Tom.
You all have turned into wonderful young men, definitely
hero material.

And to my rescuer, Steve, who set the example
for our boys.
I love you.

 SILHOUETTE BOOKS

ISBN 0-373-19394-7

HER SURPRISE FAMILY

Copyright © 1999 by Patricia Wright

Visit us at www.romance.net

Printed in U.S.A.

PATRICIA THAYER

has been writing for fourteen years and has published ten books with Silhouette. Her books have been nominated for the National Readers' Choice Award, Virginia Romance Writers of America's Holt Medallion and a prestigious RITA Award. In 1997, *Nothing Short of a Miracle* won the *Romantic Times Magazine* Reviewers' Choice Award for Best Special Edition.

Thanks to the understanding men in her life—her husband of twenty-eight years, Steve, and her three sons—Pat has been able to fulfill her dream of writing romance. Another dream is to own a cabin in Colorado, where she can spend her days writing and her evenings with her favorite hero, Steve. She loves to hear from readers. You can write her at P.O. Box 6251, Anaheim, CA 92816-0251.

WISCONSIN

MICHIGAN

Lake Michigan

Chicago •

Fort Wayne •

INDIANA

ILLINOIS

Indianapolis
★

OHIO

Bloomington •

<u>Haven Springs</u> •

Louisville •

N

KENTUCKY

All underlined places are fictitious.

Prologue

"Rafaele Mario Covelli, you come out of the water *adesso*, now," Vittoria called to her ten-year-old grandson from the back porch.

"You just ate your lunch."

The thin, lanky boy climbed out of the large swimming pool his father had assembled in the backyard for the long, hot summer months.

"But I feel fine, Nonna. I want to swim with my friends."

"You can swim a little later. You must let your food digest first."

"But I'm bored," he protested as he slumped down on the step.

"Then play with your baby sister." Nonna looked over at the precious black-haired three-year-old digging happily in her sandbox.

"No way," Rafe said. "I'm not playing with any girl."

Vittoria folded her arms and looked sternly at the boy. She knew for a fact that both Rafe and his younger brother,

Rick, loved their baby sister and played with her often. "Then come here and I'll tell you a story."

Rafe's dark eyes lit up as he sat cross-legged on his towel. "About Nonno Enrico and how he was a hero?"

Nodding, Vittoria spread out a blanket and sat on it. Little Angelina toddled over to see what was going on. She climbed on to her grandmother's lap. "You want to hear the story, too, *bambina?*"

Angelina pushed her sunbonnet back from her eyes and nodded eagerly. "Please," she said.

Before Vittoria knew it, her other grandson, Rick, and two of his school friends were seated on the blanket, too.

"Many years ago in Italy, my *famiglia,* the Perrones, lived in a small village. When I was a young girl, it was a bad time. War ravaged the countryside, but my village in Tuscany fortunately seemed to be safe. Until an airplane crashed not far from our home."

"It was Grandpa's plane. A B-24," Rafe announced. "He was a nose gunner."

Vittoria nodded. "Yes. It was an American plane. It had been hit and the pilot was trying to make it back to his base over the border, but was forced to crash-land in a field not far from our farmhouse. The next day, I found Army Sergeant Enrico Covelli hiding in our barn. He was wounded in the leg and had lost a lot of blood."

Vittoria remembered it as if it were yesterday. His face was bruised from the rough landing and he was grimacing from the pain of his wounds. He'd still been the handsomest man she'd ever seen. He was also the enemy. But she was afraid he might die, and she couldn't let that happen in her barn—or a prison camp.

"And you saved him."

Immersed in the memory now, Vittoria hardly heard her grandson's voice urge her on. "I knew I should turn him in, but I ended up caring for his wounds and sneaking out to stay with him while he fought his fever. Then after a few days, he began to get his strength back. He was American, but he spoke to me in Italiano. I was shocked when he told me his name was Enrico Covelli. His parents had come from Rome. I could not turn him over to the soldiers."

"No, Nonna," Rafe said, shaking his head, "you had to hide him."

Vittoria looked around at the other three boys as they nodded in agreement.

"But I was afraid he'd be discovered." And Vittoria had known that she was also falling in love with the American. Then came the night Enrico confessed his love for her. He didn't want to leave her, but he had to find his way back to the Allied lines. They'd both be in danger if he was caught.

She continued the story. "I'd heard about the underground—a group who helped get people to safety. The next night, before Nonno Enrico left, he promised that he would return after the war. He said he wanted to marry me and take me to America. I told him I loved him, too. Then he kissed me goodbye and disappeared into the night."

Rafe stood and leaned toward his grandmother. "Can I show them the box?" he whispered.

Vittoria nodded and Rafe hurried into the house. Within minutes he returned with a beautiful hand-carved jewelry box. He handed it to his grandmother and she opened the ornate brass clasp. She reached inside and took out the medal.

Rafe held it up. "My grandpa got a Purple Heart for being shot." There were oohs and ahhs from the boys as the medal was passed around.

"For months I never knew if Enrico ever made it to safety. Another year passed, and then the war ended." Tears filled her eyes at the memory. "I thought he must have died, because he'd promised never to forget about me."

"But he didn't die," Rafe said encouragingly.

Vittoria took her grandson's hand. "No, but I had no word from him. I still waited. By then my *padre* had arranged for me to marry Giovanni Valente."

Rafe's eyes narrowed. "But you didn't want to marry him."

"No, Rafe, I didn't love Giovanni as I loved Enrico. But my *famiglia* urged me to marry him because of his wealth. Even during the war, the Valentes managed to hold on to their vineyards. We had nothing left of value except the set of ruby rings that was to go to the firstborn daughter when she married. That was me. And my *padre* already had given the rings to Giovanni."

It still saddened her to remember it all. She had used the yards of white silk from Enrico's discarded parachute for her wedding gown. At least she'd have something of her true love with her.

"But Grandpa came back to rescue you."

Vittoria smiled. So many times she had told this story to her children and now her grandchildren. "*Si,* he returned the week of my wedding."

She recalled the day clearly. She had nearly fainted when Enrico came for her. He took her into his arms and kissed her until she realized she wasn't dreaming. He'd come back, just as he'd promised.

"Your *nonno* asked to marry me, but my *padre* insisted that I was already promised to another. That didn't stop Enrico. Together we went to the Valente *famiglia* to explain. Giovanni was furious that I wouldn't marry him, but finally agreed to release me from the promise. However, he swore he'd never love another and refused to return one of the rings. That he slipped on his little finger as a symbol of his stolen bride. Then Madre Valente placed a curse on both rings, stating that until the two were joined again, love would not be an easy road for the Covellis or their children.''

For all these years, Vittoria's heart had ached deeply. She opened the box again and took out the remaining ring. Although her Enrico had never believed in the power of the curse, Vittoria knew that something had shadowed their love over the years. She had trouble conceiving a child, but was finally blessed with two sons. And her son Rafaele almost did not make it to the altar with his bride, Maria. Could the curse be the cause of these things?

Rafe got up on his knees. ''Can I see it?''

Vittoria opened the case to display the large bloodred ruby with a circle of diamonds embedded in the ornate gold band. When the two rings had been side by side, they were a perfect pair. The last time had been more than fifty years ago.

''Wow! I bet it's worth a million dollars.''

''Oh, Rafaele. This ring is a symbol of love, and it's priceless. And true love is the only thing that will break the curse and bring the two rings together again.''

Chapter One

More than one hundred years old, and Stewart Manor was still a sight to behold.

Rafe Covelli drove his truck through the wrought-iron gates and gazed at the three-story structure. Years ago this place had been one of Haven Springs's most regal homes. Even the missing shingles and peeling trim paint couldn't take away from the grandeur of the architecture.

Ever since he'd been a kid, it had fascinated him. He'd ridden by on his bike and stared at the big, haunted-looking house, wondering what it would be like to live in such a place. His imagination had dreamed up all sorts of secret passages, hidden rooms and a few ghosts.

None of it was true, of course. The grand house had been built for wealthy businessman William Stewart, who had been mayor of Haven Springs at the turn of the century. His son, William, Jr., and his wife had lived here along with their only child, a daughter named Hannah. As a boy, Rafe remembered nice Miss Hannah, who'd never married and lived in the house until her death three years ago.

A distant cousin inherited the estate, but not wanting the big house, he put Stewart Manor up for auction. The town's landmark sold for a fraction of its worth. This was the first time someone other than a Stewart was going to live there.

Rafe stopped his truck in front of the house and noticed the woman standing on the porch. It looked like he was about to meet Haven Springs's newest resident, Ms. Shelby Harris.

Grabbing his clipboard, he climbed out of the cab. He made his way up the walkway, flanked by overgrown weeds, to the porch steps.

"Ms. Harris?" He tipped his baseball cap with the Covelli and Sons logo. "I'm Rafe Covelli."

The woman appeared to be in her late twenties. She nodded. "Thank you for coming by, Mr. Covelli."

"No problem. I've been working in the area. We're doing the facade restoration on the houses up the street."

When Rafe climbed the steps, he was surprised to find that the woman was nearly eye to eye with him. He was over six feet, so Shelby Harris had to be at least five-ten. A quick glance told him her height was all in a pair of long, slender legs, encased right now in a pair of nicely fitted jeans. His gaze moved to her narrow waist, then to the cotton T-shirt that did little to hide full breasts. His pulse began to race in appreciation. It had been a while since a stranger this appealing had come to town. The last had been Jill Morgan, who recently married his younger brother, Rick. Rafe's gaze moved to her oval face, framed by short brown curls, and his heart did a somersault as he met the most incredible green eyes he'd ever seen.

His scrutiny seemed to make her nervous and she glanced away. "As I told you on the phone, I plan to turn Stewart Manor into a bed-and-breakfast inn."

Rafe let out a low whistle. "And I explained that was going to take some work. And money."

"I'm not afraid of work, Mr. Covelli," she said. "But if you can't handle the job..."

The woman was prickly as a cactus. "I didn't say I couldn't handle the job." He stepped off the porch and squinted into the bright August sun, looking up at the massive structure, then began to calculate the things that needed immediate attention. The gables along the top story were badly in need of repair—the wood was weathered and rotted in some places. That was Rick's specialty; maybe he could drag his brother out here to do the job. The roof was in bad shape and needed to be replaced. That meant the inside had to have rain damage.

He glanced back at her. "How much time and money do you have, Ms. Harris?"

"That's what I want to talk to you about."

The look on her face told him he was in trouble. Damn. He'd seen that same expression on his sister's face too many times. This was serious. Something was up and he wasn't sure he wanted to know what. "Okay, talk."

Her back straightened stubbornly. "Most of my ready cash went into buying this house. It will be a month or so before I have more available. Right now I need to be a little frugal. I thought maybe we could work out some sort of...deal."

Rafe knew he should turn around, climb back into his truck and drive off. He had enough of his own problems without giving away his time. But something kept him rooted to the spot. Maybe he was curious about why a single woman wanted to buy this old house and turn it into a bed-and-breakfast. And the longing in her sparkling eyes made him ask, "What do you have in mind?"

Shelby stepped into the sun, which brought out the coppery highlights in her dark hair. "Because of the historical status of this house, all the facade repair is covered under the federal grant money."

Rafe nodded. "We're already handling that."

"Yes, I've seen your work around town. You're very good. But I need more done. I would like you to check the roof and have a look at the front rooms inside. Tell me how much it would cost to fix it up—" she hesitated and took a deep breath "—a little at a time. The bare necessities. Enough so I can open for business."

Rafe held back his smile. "Haven Springs isn't exactly overflowing with tourists."

"But with the summer there's the lake traffic, and then in the fall people come to see the foliage. I plan to advertise—there are people who like to stay in historical homes. After a few months I'll be able to afford to continue the work on restoring Stewart Manor."

There was that stubborn attitude again. Her full mouth drew into a pouty bow and something stirred in his gut. Damn.

"Let's have a look, then." He returned to the porch and walked to the heavy oak door with its oval cut-glass center. He opened it and stepped over the threshold into a huge entryway. A dim coolness greeted him as he stood on the bare hardwood floors. A magnificent chandelier hung from the high ceiling, edged with oak crown molding. The staircase across the hall made its way to the second story. Several spindles were missing in the banister, and a few of the steps were also missing.

"You'd better stay off the stairs until I've checked them out," he said as he turned to his left and entered the front room, what used to be called the parlor.

Shelby stood back and watched the cocky Mr. Covelli move around her house. So he thought she was helpless. That she had to be warned about obvious dangers. Well, she had news for him. She'd spent her entire life taking care of herself and could do it just fine.

She'd asked around and knew he was her best chance for a fair deal. Worse, he knew it, too.

She went after him only to find him standing at the three double-hung windows and eying the frames. Then he glanced down at the ornate woodwork along the baseboards. He squatted for a closer look. She couldn't help but notice the nice curve of his rear end, the way his muscular thighs strained against the fabric of his worn jeans. Her gaze moved to his chambray shirt as the muscles of his broad shoulders and back flexed. A shiver of awareness raced through her. She quickly raised her eyes to his face and found him in deep concentration. His bronze skin bespoke his Italian ancestry and the fact that he worked in the sun.

His eyes were chocolate brown and mesmerizing. His coal-black hair was cropped short around the ears. He pulled off his cap and his thick mane still appeared neatly combed. She somehow knew that was the way Rafe Covelli's life was. All in neat, organized order. Everything cut and dried. Black or white.

The complete opposite of hers.

She doubted he would go along with her idea. It was beginning to seem crazy even to her.

"Well, Ms. Harris," he said as he stood and faced her, "there's bad news. You've had a water leak around these two west windows." He pointed out the spots.

Shelby's gaze was glued to his large hand with the long, tapered fingers. Strong, capable hands that carved wood. She couldn't help but wonder how the roughened palms would feel on her skin.... She blinked away the thought and turned her attention back to what he was saying.

"First, I'll have to go up to the attic and find the leaks, then I'll have to replace these frames and tear out the plaster." He went down on one knee. "See the moisture here? It's worked down into the baseboards. This section of wood is warped and will have to be replaced, too." He stood and walked into the hall again. She hurried to keep up. "The stairway needs to have those steps and spindles replaced. All in top-grade oak." He kept walking until he finally reached the living room.

This was the room where Shelby had taken up residence. She'd cleaned and hung curtains, then arranged her furniture which consisted of a sofa, a chair, a portable television and a bookcase. A desk and computer were against the far wall. The only other rooms she'd used since moving in three days ago, had been the small servants' quarters off the kitchen, which consisted of a bedroom and bath.

Rafe approached the huge stone fireplace and began to check out the carved-oak mantel. She held her breath when he stopped and eyed the framed photographs lined up on the top.

He looked at her. "Family?" he asked.

Shelby hesitated, then answered, "Yes."

He smiled. "I didn't think anyone had more family than I do."

He studied the assortment of pictures, and a wave of envy washed over her. Like most people, Rafe Covelli seemed to take his relatives for granted. *But there are those of us who don't have a real family to claim.*

She shook away the rush of loneliness. "You have a big family, Mr. Covelli?"

He nodded. "A grandmother, a mother, a brother and sister, but also a large assortment of aunts and uncles and cousins. Family reunions are a madhouse." He smiled as his gaze met hers. Like a magnet, his dark eyes held her captive, and for a moment she couldn't breathe. Finally he turned away and moved on to finish his appraisal.

He leaned down and examined the floor. Then wrote more notes on his clipboard. "Do any of your family live around here?"

"Uh, no," she said. "They're farther south."

He glanced over his shoulder. "Why didn't you buy a house there? Then maybe your family would be able to help you out."

"I'd rather do this on my own. Besides, I could afford this place."

"How'd you find out about Stewart Manor?"

She hadn't had to answer this many questions to take out a mortgage. "It was on the Internet. You can find anything and everything if you know where to search."

Rafe stood and walked over to the corner window. "As far as I'm concerned, you can put all the computers in a pile and blow them to kingdom come."

Shelby bit back a smile as she watched the big man move around the room. So Mr. Macho was a cyberphobe. "Sounds like you've had some problems with your computer."

"None whatsoever," he assured her. "I don't touch the thing. I leave all the computer business to my sister. Angelina minored in computer science in college. Got one in the office and I stay clear of it."

"Well, if you ever decide you want to learn, just call me. I'm on the computer every day. I do graphics work and design web pages for a living."

He cocked an eyebrow as if to say, *I'll want to learn when hell freezes over.* "Thanks for the offer, but I doubt I'll ever require your services. How many rooms upstairs?"

"Five bedrooms and two baths. One of the baths is connected to the master suite. The third floor is the attic."

"How many rooms do you want me to look at?"

She shrugged. "I'd like you to tell me if any of them need major work. There are some water rings on the ceilings in two of the bedrooms, and in one of them some of the plaster has already fallen. I want to start painting and wallpapering as soon as possible."

"I think you better hold off on any decorating until we assess the damage. Tearing out old plaster causes quite a mess." His dark eyes lifted to meet hers, and instantly she felt a jolt of awareness course through her body. Why did this man make her so nervous?

She managed a nod.

"I'll go have a look." He started out of the room and again she followed him. When they reached the staircase, he stopped. She didn't and ran into him. He reached out and grabbed her by the arms before she lost her balance. "You better stay down here. These stairs aren't safe. And until the repairs are done, I don't want you using them."

Shelby felt the sudden heat from his gentle touch and lost any desire to argue. Then he turned and continued up the stairs. She watched as he moved with easy athletic grace over the broken steps. Finally he disappeared from view, and she returned to the living room.

Shelby crossed to the mantel and studied the row of pictures. Her family. Uncle Ray and Aunt Celia, along with an assortment of cousins. They were spread all across the country, of course. That way people didn't ask why they never came to visit. All she had to do was make up stories about them. And she was really good at make-believe—she made a living at it. Shelby drew a long breath and released it. She glanced around the room, feeling a flood of contentment.

She finally had her home. And soon it would be filled with people, and she wouldn't be all alone anymore.

After checking the attic and the other bedrooms, Rafe wandered into the huge master suite. A mahogany four-poster bed sat against the wall. Heavy brocade draperies hung at the large windows, but were so filthy you couldn't tell what color they'd once been. The floral wallpaper was faded and had water rings. There was also evidence of some vandalism, broken windows and beer bottles and some writing on the wallpaper. The floors were caked with years of dust.

He peeked into the bathroom and saw the oversize clawfoot tub. Upon close examination, he realized it was still in good condition, along with the pedestal sink. The marine-blue marble tile could use a good cleaning and some grouting, but all were easy to repair.

Rafe's thoughts turned to the woman he'd left downstairs. He normally didn't stop homeowners from following him around on the job site, but he needed time away from Ms. Harris. Her wide-eyed gaze seemed to watch his every move. He couldn't decide if it was mistrust or just plain curiosity. But it had bothered him. Damn. He hadn't felt that awkward around a woman since he'd taken Lisa Southerland to the junior prom. And that was because he had gotten brave enough to try to cop a feel. At seventeen, getting his hands on a girl's breasts was a major accomplishment.

Once again he recalled Shelby Harris in her T-shirt. She had an unbelievable body. Full breasts, long, shapely legs... Rafe groaned. What was the matter with him? He was acting as if he'd never been around a woman before. But it had been a while since there'd been anyone in his life. Still, he knew better than to think about getting involved with a potential client.

After giving himself a good talking-to, he returned to the bedroom. He stopped short when he found Shelby Harris in front of the bay windows. The afternoon sunlight formed a halo around her, softening her pretty face.

A quiet intimacy surrounded them as they stood in silence, neither, it seemed, wanting to break the spell with words. Rafe's gaze shifted slightly toward the large bed, and an erotic picture of this long-legged brunette lying naked on ivory satin sheets flashed in his head.

His body tightened as his gaze darted back to her. Damnation. "Thought I told you to wait downstairs."

She didn't seem intimidated by his anger. "I've been up here before. I know which steps to avoid."

"You still could have fallen. This house is old and has been vacant for a long time. If I'm going to work here, then you're going to have to listen to my warnings."

Her eyes flashed defiantly, as if she was about to argue, but then she averted her gaze. "I guess I was anxious to see how much damage you found and what your bid was going to be."

Rafe looked at his clipboard. He knew that the house needed a lot of time-consuming work. "On the whole, the house is solidly built. I think you already knew that."

She nodded.

"But the roof had been leaking for quite a few years. I was going to suggest that you replace it, but there are several bundles of shingles in the attic, so we might be able to do a fairly good patch job—for now. Once we stop the leaks, I'll tear out the ceiling up here in the front bedroom. Then put up new drywall."

"What about the other three bedrooms and this room?"

"The damage isn't extensive. This room seems to be in the best shape, and the bathroom is fine, too."

"So between the parlor downstairs, the stairway and the bedroom room, what do you think it'll cost me?"

He didn't know why, but he'd worked to cut his quote to the bare bones. He showed her the bid and watched her eyes widen.

"This is so expensive. You can't possibly need that much material."

"It's not the materials. It's the labor. I have to pay a guy to come in and tear away and dispose of the rotted wood and plaster."

"No, you don't."

"Well, someone has to do it. And I don't have the time. My brother and I have several other jobs—"

"I know," she interrupted. "I know you're busy. That's the reason I'm suggesting that, instead of hiring someone to do the tearing out, let me do it. I can work along with you."

Rafe knew it. The minute he'd pulled into the driveway, he'd had a feeling she wanted more than an estimate.

Well, he had to set her straight. "Look, you have no idea what is involved with this. It's hard, backbreaking work." He eyed her slender body. "I have trouble finding high-school boys willing to do this kind of labor."

"But this is my home," she said. "I have a lot invested in it already. And right now I don't have enough funds left to get this place ready to open for business."

"Could your family help you?"

She glanced away. "I'm too old to go running to family for money."

He looked around. "This is a big project, Ms. Harris. Maybe your parents would like to invest in making this place at least livable for their daughter."

Her hands curled into fists. "My parents aren't able to help out, Mr. Covelli. And for your information, this house was inspected before the auction. The gas company deemed the stove in the kitchen safe to use. The plumbing was checked out and fixed before I bought the house. So you see, this place is very livable. But if you won't help me, then I'll find another contractor who will."

She pulled a business card out of her pocket. "There's…the Norton Construction Company in Bedford," she read. "So, thank you for your time." She turned and headed out to the hall.

"Norton Construction? They have a reputation for doing things cheap, but you won't get the quality this house deserves." He went after her as she approached the stairs.

"It's what I can afford, Mr. Covelli."

He reached her side. "Will you please stop calling me that? You make me feel ancient. My name is Rafe."

She stopped and swung around. "What I call you isn't going to change the fact that I can't afford you."

Rafe could see the sheen of tears in her eyes, then she turned away and put her tennis-shoe-clad foot on the next step. One of the weakened steps. A scream erupted from her lips as she lost her balance and began to fall.

Rafe caught her and managed to halt her progress. He yanked her against him, and they both went down hard on one of the steps. Shelby ended up lying on top of him, his arms wrapped around her tightly. She felt incredible. Her softness against his hardness. He inhaled her fresh flowery scent. Suddenly his body caught fire and he knew he had to let her go.

But he couldn't move.

Shelby finally pushed herself up and looked at him with those remarkable green eyes. He stifled a groan as his gaze moved to her mouth; he was unable to ignore how badly he wanted a taste.

He blinked away his wayward thoughts. "Are you all right?"

Blushing, she nodded and got off him. "I guess I wasn't watching where I was going."

"It happens. But you can see why you need to get these stairs fixed before someone really gets hurt."

"Yes, I do." She sat down on the step. "And I will. Thank you for coming by with your bid."

He got up. He started down the stairs, but knew he couldn't leave her to Gus Norton. "Look, I can give you the names of other reliable companies, but the cost won't be any less than my bid." He wrote down two names on a piece of paper and handed it to her.

She took it. "I appreciate it. Thank you."

He stood there for a few seconds. Even though this woman was tall, she had a delicate build and would have a hard time moving heavy materials, but from what he saw in the thirty minutes of knowing her, Shelby Harris was stubborn enough to try.

"I'll have a crew here on Wednesday to start the work outside," he said.

She nodded, but didn't smile. And for some reason he was disappointed. After all, he was doing her a favor.

"Look, if I get a bit of time, maybe I could help you tear out—"

"I don't need your charity, Mr. Covelli," she said stubbornly. "I'll get it done."

"I don't doubt that, Ms. Harris, but I wasn't offering charity. Here in Haven Springs we call it being neighborly."

Chapter Two

Shelby stood on the front porch watching Rafe's Chevy truck pull out of the drive onto the quiet, tree-lined street.

"Arrogant man," she mumbled as she sat down on one of the steps. What right did he have to boss her around? No man was going to tell her what to do. She wasn't her mother, weak and submissive, allowing men to control her life, then walk out on her. As a child, she remembered the men who'd come and gone from Nola Harris's life, including Shelby's father. Years ago she had vowed she'd never let a man get close enough to hurt her.

Well, she had managed most of her life just fine by herself, and Rafe Covelli wasn't going to change that.

Shelby glanced behind her at the house, and suddenly she was overwhelmed. How was she going to get all of it done? She sighed tiredly, remembering how hard she'd worked and saved for this place. Now this was her home. Excitement raced through her. Stewart Manor was hers.

She turned and surveyed the vast lawn. It wasn't so much grass as two acres of knee-high weeds. The dozen or so maple trees could stand to be trimmed. So could the hedge that lined the wrought-iron fence bordering the property.

She stood and went down the steps, refusing to let herself get depressed. All her life she'd managed to handle anything that had been tossed at her, and she'd survived. With this place there was a lot to do, but she could handle it.

Making her way to the rear of the house, she realized that this area wasn't in any better shape than the front. Weeds were everywhere. The large rose garden had been neglected, but there were some bushes that had survived the neglect.

Shelby continued her inspection of the property and followed the old brick walkway past a row of trees. She froze at the sight of a little cottage, its paint peeling and most of its windows broken. Taking a deep breath to calm her racing heart, she kept moving through the high grass toward the building.

A rusty glider swing sat on the small porch, which made memories flood her head. A hot Indiana summer, and she and her mom sitting on that very swing, waiting for rain to cool things off. Shelby had only been six years old, but that period in her life had been tucked neatly into her heart as the happiest time she'd ever spent with her mother. The last summer they were together—before Nola went away.

She felt a chill course through her, and her emotions threatened to surface. She was unable to stop the recollection of the nice woman who used to come and visit them at the cottage. A woman who lived in Stewart Manor and her name was Miss Hannah. She was pretty and always smiling. When she visited in the evenings, she'd bring cookies or ice cream. One time she brought a doll.

Then one night when Miss Hannah came by, Nola sent her daughter to bed.

But that didn't stop Shelby from hearing their argument. The next day, Nola packed up their shabby suitcases and they left Stewart Manor. A bus took them away, and her mother never explained why.

Not long after that, Nola hooked up with another man, Orin Harris. Nola said he was going to be her daddy. Shelby didn't want a daddy, especially someone who was mean to her mother. Besides, Orin and Nola were always drunk and at night they'd fight. One day her mother had gotten sick, and with no other relatives to take Shelby, she had been put in foster care. She never saw or heard from her mother again. Later she was told she had died.

Shelby was almost overcome with sadness. But she drew a shaky breath and fought it, as she had so many times. Denial was her protection against getting hurt.

"Hello, is anyone there?"

With a startled gasp, Shelby jerked around to find an old man standing in the rose arbor. He was short, and as he walked toward her, she noticed he had a slight limp. He had snowy white hair and a ruddy complexion, and his smile let her know he wasn't a threat.

"May I help you?" Shelby asked.

"I'm Ely Cullen, ma'am." He held out his hand.

She shook it and felt his work-hardened hand. "Hello, Ely. I'm Shelby Harris."

"I know. The town's been buzzing about the new owner of Stewart Manor. I was down at the hardware store earlier when I thought I should come by to welcome you to town." He glanced around and sighed. "It sure was a fine place in its day." His hazel eyes returned to her. "Could be again."

"It's going to take a long time and a lot of money," Shelby said. "But I plan to turn the manor into a bed-and-breakfast."

Ely nodded. "Could you use some help getting the grounds in shape?"

Shelby's spirits soared. "I'd love it. But right now all I can afford are these two hands." She held them up.

"What if you didn't have to pay?"

Shelby paused and eyed the old man closely. She didn't like to take handouts. And he couldn't possibly handle the hot, humid summer weather. "That's awfully nice of you, Mr. Cullen, but this is a big job."

"I know. I did it for over thirty years."

She stared at the man. "You were the gardener for Stewart Manor?"

He nodded happily. "I used to prune Miss Hannah's prize-winning roses. Mowed the lawns and trimmed all the hedges. Now I know I'm older and slower these days, but it's been hard for me to stand by and watch the place go downhill since Miss Hannah's passing." His eyes raised to Shelby's. "I can still be useful."

"You sure? I could really use the help, Ely, but I don't want you to be overworked."

"I won't, 'cause I'm going to bring my grandson with me to do the heavy stuff."

"Then I have to insist on paying him."

He smiled. "We'll work something out. Right now let's just spruce up the place a little."

"I want that as badly as you do," Shelby said, finally feeling as if things were going in her favor.

Later that afternoon Rafe walked into Maria's Ristorante and sat down at the end of the bar in the section reserved for Maria's family.

He was a little early for dinner, but he wanted to talk to his brother, Rick, and this was the best place to find him. Rick's wife, Jill, had agreed to work the afternoon shift until she began her teaching job in the fall. The two had only been married a month and they were inseparable.

Rafe envied his brother. Rick had found love, and more importantly, he hadn't been afraid to go after what he wanted. That had been Jill. Rafe hadn't had time to find and court a wife. Not that he'd wanted one.

If the Covelli curse wasn't enough to deter Rafe from finding love, he'd had plenty to handle since his father's accident and death two years ago. Being the eldest son, Rafe had been responsible for Nonna Vittoria, his mother, Maria, and sister, Angelina. And he couldn't forget the family construction business, Covelli and Sons. Things had gone sour when his father's accident had been blamed on substandard materials, and Rafaele Covelli, Sr., had been the contractor for the building. It had taken a few months, but with the help of Rick and their cousin Tony, Rafe had gotten the business back on track. They were still searching for the creeps responsible for the accident, and Rafe vowed he wasn't going to stop until he'd cleared his father's name.

Recently the family had branched out into different business ventures and were doing well. They even had enough work to employ a bigger crew. But Covelli and Sons had never been about quantity. It was quality that counted, and Rafe had always been the best custom carpenter he could be. His dad taught him that.

That was why he'd laid down the law to Shelby Harris. He remembered the way he'd left her on the porch of Stewart Manor. Her long, jean-clad legs, her emerald-green eyes… Why did he feel as if he'd deserted her?

Because he knew Gus Norton did shoddy work. That man was quick to cut corners. Rafe hated the thought of Gus laying his grimy hand on any of the beautiful woodwork in that house.

"Hey, bro."

Rafe turned to see Rick coming toward him carrying Jill's son, Lucas. The eighteen-month-old boy grinned and reached out for his newly acquired uncle.

Rafe took the boy and sat him on the bar. "Hello, Lucas."

"Hi," Lucas said, acting shy.

Rafe looked at his brother. "I take it you're both visiting a certain pretty blond waitress."

"Yeah," Rick said as his gaze wandered over to where Jill waited on a table. "It's tough having her at work all day."

"Poor thing." He tickled his nephew's chin. "Most people have to work for a living."

"Hey, I work," Rick said. "I've been replacing the hardwood flooring in the living room at the house." He was talking about the Victorian home on Ash Street that he and Jill had bought a few months back. After moving in a month ago, they'd decided to take their time and redo each room. So far they'd finished the kitchen, master bedroom and Lucas's room.

"I ran into another fixer upper today. Shelby Harris."

"She's the one who bought the big old Stewart place?"

"Yeah. She plans on opening a bed-and-breakfast. It's a mess right now. You could spend months working on that place. But the craftsmanship is incredible. Dad would have loved it."

"Didn't he do some work there when we were kids?"

Rafe nodded. "He designed kitchen cabinets for Mrs. Stewart about twenty years ago. I didn't go in the kitchen today."

"So what are you doing for this Ms. Harris?"

"Nothing."

Rick frowned. "She didn't like your ugly mug?"

"I was too expensive for her. I think she overextended herself buying the place. Not enough money left over to do any restoring. I don't think she had any idea what it would cost in time and materials." He shook his head. "That's one stubborn woman."

"Ohh, so you've noticed she's a woman. That's good. Is she young? Old? Pretty?"

Rafe shrugged. "She's about our age, and I didn't pay any attention to what she looked like," he lied.

"Oh, no. You are in trouble, bro, if you can't remember whether or not she's pretty. You've been too long without female companionship."

Rafe gave him a pointed look. "When have I had time? I've been trying to keep the business together."

"And doing a wonderful job, I might add." Rick opened a package of bread sticks and gave one to Lucas. "I hope you know how much I appreciated your keeping things going while I was away all those years."

Rafe knew the guilt his younger brother felt for joining the marines, then going to Texas to find his fortune in oil, rather than staying home to work in the family business.

"I wanted the business to keep going—for dad. We don't have to worry about our independent mom, because she has the restaurant. But Covelli and Sons is our legacy." It was more than that to Rafe. He remembered his father teaching him about woodworking when he was a child and talking about his sons someday joining the business. Rafe had wanted nothing more than to become an expert carpenter like his father, the man he was named after.

Rick broke into his thoughts. "Well, now it looks like you have more than enough to keep busy," Rick said. "Charlie told me you're about ready to rent out the store-front offices."

Rafe nodded. "I'm putting the ad in next week for that space and also the three low-income apartments upstairs. If you hadn't been off fixing up your own house, you could keep up with these things." He turned to his little nephew. "Right, kid?"

Lucas nodded. "Right."

Rick smiled. "Things have sure turned around these past few months. From the verge of bankruptcy to showing a profit in seven months. Good old cousin Tony was unbelievable coming up with the idea of purchasing the store-fronts downtown and restoring them." He gave his brother a sideways glance. "Too bad we couldn't get Stewart Manor. Restoring a place like that would be wonderful advertising for the business."

Rafe shook his head. "What did you want me to do? Give away our services? I doubt she can even afford materials."

"Maybe something could be worked out. Sounds like this Ms. Harris needs to fix the place up so she can open for business."

"Maybe she should have taken out a larger loan."

Rick remained silent.

"So I'm the bad guy here," Rafe said.

"Bad boy," Lucas chimed in.

Rick laughed at his son's antics. Lucas joined in and clapped his hands. Hearing the commotion, Jill Covelli wandered over to the bar. She smiled and her blue eyes shone as she looked up at her new husband. She and Rick exchanged a look that made Rafe almost believe in love.

"What's so funny?" she asked, and took the time to kiss her husband and son.

"My older brother's got woman trouble."

Jill smiled. "Who is she?"

"The new owner of Stewart Manor," Rick said.

"Oh, you mean Shelby Harris. I saw her at the bank the other day. Mrs. Kerrigan pointed her out to me. A pretty brunette, tall and slender."

"With the most incredible green eyes," Rafe said before he could stop himself.

"Looks like another one is about to bite the dust," Rick said, grinning.

Rafe shook his head. "Oh, no. I'm not as brave as you, bro. I'm not about to mess around with the Covelli curse."

Around six o'clock Wednesday morning Shelby awoke to the sound of men's voices outside. She rolled over and realized she'd fallen asleep on the sofa while going over some work. She got up and went to the window. Pulling back the curtain, she looked out to find Rafe Covelli standing on her lawn along with two men. One was an older man of maybe forty-five, the other about the same size and age as Rafe.

It took a minute before Shelby remembered that Rafe Covelli was starting work on the front this morning. Her attention was drawn to how good Rafe looked in his navy T-shirt with his broad shoulders and muscular chest. Her gaze lowered to his faded jeans. His legs and rear end weren't bad either.

Suddenly Rafe turned and saw her at the window. Their eyes connected and held for what seemed like a long time. Finally Shelby realized she was in her pajamas. She dropped the curtain and hurried to get dressed. After pulling on a pair of jeans, she grabbed a white T-shirt from her dresser and slipped her feet into a pair of beat-up tennis shoes. She finger-combed her short hair and went outside.

The sun made her squint, and she shielded her eyes from the sun as she approached Rafe.

"Morning," he said sternly. "Sorry to wake you, but we need to get started before it gets too hot."

"I understand. I'm usually up, but I was working late on the computer." Shelby looked at the man standing next to Rafe.

"Hi, I'm Rick Covelli. The rude guy's my brother. Sorry we didn't warn you we were coming so early."

"No problem. Like I said, I just overslept this morning."

"Well, we'll be as quiet as possible. I just need to check out the gables." Rick glanced up at the huge brick structure. "I have to admit that I'm anxious to get my hands on this place. Mind if I go upstairs to have a look?"

"Sure. Go right ahead."

Rick tipped his baseball cap. "Nice meeting you, Shelby.

And welcome to Haven Springs. I hope you're going to like it here."

"I'm sure I will."

"Our mother asked us to extend you an invitation to stop by the restaurant—Maria's Ristorante. She and my *nonna* would like to meet you. My wife, Jill, also works there."

Shelby's head was spinning. She couldn't believe these too men were brothers. One was open and friendly, the other brooding. She glanced at Rafe, who was busy writing something on his clipboard. "That would be nice, Rick. I've been pretty busy with moving in and trying to catch up on my work. I run a computer-graphics business from the house."

Rick smiled again. "Interesting work. Just don't let Rafe anywhere close to your machine. He and computers don't get along."

Rafe glared at his brother. "Don't you thinks it's about time you started working, bro?"

"All right," Rick said cheerfully, heading for the house. "I'll be on the third floor if you need anything."

Rafe introduced the older man as Charlie. Then another truck pulled into the driveway. It bore the logo of Norton Construction.

Shelby ignored Rafe's look as she walked toward the man getting out of the truck. "Hello, I'm Shelby Harris," she said, and shook his hand. "You must be Gus." The man appeared to be in his late thirties. He was heavyset and evidently hadn't taken the time to shave. And although it was early morning, his clothes were already dirty.

"Howdy, ma'am," Gus Norton said. He looked around. "I see Covelli is doing your exterior." He shook his head. "I don't blame you for not accepting his inflated prices. Old Gus here, I can do it for you at a lower cost. I'll fix up the old Stewart place for ya."

Shelby knew she was making a mistake. "Like I said on

the phone, Mr. Norton, I can't afford to do much right now.''

He nodded and gave her a wicked grin. "That's right, sweetheart. You said you wanted to work something out.''

Shelby cringed. Asking for a bid from this man had been a mistake.

"Well, hey there, Rafe,'' Gus said. "I hear you're doing these facade renovations. It's a shame you had to get out of new construction because of what happened to your daddy.''

"I'm doing exactly what I want to be doing, Norton,'' Rafe said coldly.

Shelby could only stand back and watch the sparks fly between the two men. Then Charlie leaped into the fray. "Since when did they allow you inside the city limits, Norton?''

Gus just grinned. "Hey, Charlie. You ever want to work in real construction again, give me a call.''

Charlie started to say something, but he glanced at Shelby and seemed to think better of it. He walked away.

Shelby quickly ushered Gus into the house and sent him off to his task. In the kitchen she made a pot of coffee. She needed the caffeine to get her going this morning.

She'd spent most of the previous evening at the computer, trying to hammer out the ideas that were due tomorrow. She'd been behind with her work since she'd come to Haven Springs.

With her business doing so well, it had been a bad time to do the move from Louisville, but she couldn't wait to get into her new home. Now she was paying for it. If she didn't finish the story she'd been working on in time, she wouldn't get paid—and she desperately needed the money for the restoration of her new home.

Home. The word seemed strange to her. In her almost twenty-nine years she'd never been able to call anyplace home.

"I can't believe you actually went ahead and called that guy for a bid."

Shelby turned around to find Rafe Covelli standing in the doorway.

"I told you, Mr. Covelli, that I needed to get some things done on this house. The rains don't stop just because I can't afford to fix the roof."

"I'll fix the roof. You already have enough materials in the attic for a decent patch job. I could have it done in a few days. Then you can take your time on some of the other repairs. Just don't hire that jerk upstairs. Believe me, he doesn't know a router from a chisel."

Shelby was tempted to smile but didn't. She was curious to know why Rafe Covelli was coming to her rescue. Or maybe she shouldn't ask why and just accept it. "I won't take charity. I'm going to pay you."

"You can pay me by getting that jerk who calls himself a contractor out of this house. Stewart Manor deserves the best. That's me." Rafe entered the kitchen and stopped, eyeing the oak cabinets.

Shelby smiled. "They're beautiful, aren't they? But I don't think they're part of the original house."

Rafe ran his hand over the fine wood grain. "No, they weren't. They were put in about twenty years ago."

"How do you know that?"

"Because my dad did the work." He said this with such pride that she envied him his childhood and the obvious love and respect he had for his father.

"The cabinets are my favorite thing in this kitchen," she said.

He turned to her. "And if you love this house as much as I think you do, get rid of Norton."

"Stop giving me orders, Mr. Covelli."

"It's Rafe."

Shelby swallowed as she looked into his intense dark eyes.

"What do you say, Shelby? Do we have a deal? I'll do the repairs on the roof if you tell Gus to get lost."

"I told you I won't take your charity. Maybe we can trade something."

A twinkle appeared in his eyes and she rushed on to suggest, "How about I teach you about computers?"

He blinked. "You've got to be kidding."

"Take it or leave it," Shelby said.

Rafe couldn't believe this was happening. He was bargaining to get the privilege to repair her roof. When had he lost the upper hand here? But it was worth it when Shelby went upstairs to find Gus Norton and told him the bad news.

Just as she returned to the kitchen, a teenage boy came rushing to the back door. "Miss Harris. Miss Harris."

Shelby dashed outside, Rafe following. "What is it, Josh?"

"It's my grandfather. I think he fell." The boy pointed to the yard.

Shelby hurried across the lawn. Rafe was right behind her. When they reached the rose garden, they found Ely Cullen lying on the ground.

"Don't move him," Rafe said. He knelt down beside the man. "Ely, can you hear me?"

"Of course I can hear you." The old man tried to get up. "I just lost my balance. Bum knee gave out." He sat up with help from Rafe.

"Wait. Let me check to see if anything is broken."

"Ain't nothin' broken—just my pride."

"Maybe I should take you to the doctor just in case," Rafe suggested as he pulled out a handkerchief and dabbed at the scratch on Ely's head. "Does anything hurt?"

"Son, at my age something always hurts."

"Grandpa, maybe you should go. You have scratches on your face and arm." The blond teenager looked concerned.

"Josh, I fell on the grass. I'm fine. Like I said, my knee gave out. Just need a little help getting up."

Rafe eased the man to his feet. The old man did seem steady enough. "Ely, what are you doing out here at seven in the morning?"

"I'm working for Miss Shelby. We're going to get the lawn and garden in shape by the end of the summer."

Rafe had had just about enough. Shelby Harris had hired the area's worst contractor, and then a seventy-seven-year-old man to help with the yard work. He assisted Ely into a lawn chair.

"I'll get you a glass of water," Shelby said.

Rafe stopped her. "I think, to be on the safe side, we should run Ely to the clinic."

"I don't need to go," Ely argued.

Rafe exchanged a worried glance with Shelby. She swallowed hard and he could see her fear. "Please, Ely. I'd feel better if you were checked out. I am responsible for your safety, after all."

The older man smiled. "It wasn't your fault."

Shelby wanted to kiss the old man. "I know it wasn't. It wasn't anyone's. But an accident happened." Oh, Lord, she thought, what if he really was hurt?

"Okay, I'll go to the doctor as long as this doesn't mean I can't work in the garden."

"If the doctor says it's okay, you can work here all you want."

"I'll get the truck," Rafe said, and rushed off.

Shelby watched him go, knowing that Rafe Covelli was going to give her a lecture over this one. But right now all she cared about was getting Ely taken care of.

Chapter Three

Shelby sat in the Mayfair Clinic waiting room with Josh. As she anxiously waited for news, she played a few games of hearts and thumbed through every old magazine on the table.

"I promised my dad I'd watch Grandpa. I'm sorry, Miss Harris."

"Call me, Shelby, Josh. And I'm not blaming you for anything. It was an accident. We just have to watch your grandfather more closely."

"He isn't going to lose his job, is he? Ever since he came home two days ago telling us about the new owner of Stewart Manor, all he's talked about is working in Miss Hannah's garden again. I haven't seen him so happy in a long time. If I promise to stay with him, can he still work?"

"Of course. I'd love to have Ely working at the house. His gardening experience is a valuable asset."

Just then Rafe and Ely came down the hall. Ely had a bandage on his forehead. She and Josh both went to them. "Are you okay, Grandpa?"

Shelby looked at Rafe for verification. "Ely is fine. The doctor said he's got a few bruises and scratches. He just put a little too much strain on his bad knee."

"It's the pits being old," Ely said. "You feel so dang useless."

"You aren't useless, Ely. Your skills are priceless. Just don't overdo." She surprised herself and grasped both his hands. "I don't want anything to happen to you."

The older man nodded. "I'll have Josh do the hard physical work."

"You just go slower," Shelby suggested. "And concentrate on the rose garden. I think I can scrape together enough to have some men come in and do the mowing and trimming."

Ely grinned. "I know a few men who could use a little money, and if I supervise, it'll get done right."

Shelby turned to Rafe and found a pleased look on his face. "How about we go to lunch and discuss it?" he asked. "My treat."

When they all started out the door, Shelby hung back to talk with Rafe. "You don't need to take us to lunch. I can handle that. I'm paying."

"Fine. You try and convince my mother to take your money."

"I will," she said, determinedly. "And I'm responsible for Ely's doctor bill, too. How much was it?"

Rafe kept walking. "I'll just add it to whatever else you owe me."

"I owe you nothing," she insisted in a hushed tone.

"The patch job on the roof," he reminded her.

"I thought we were doing a trade. I was going to teach you how to use a computer."

Rafe frowned. "Get real, Ms. Harris. I have no desire to learn about computers."

"*You* get real, Mr. Covelli. This is the computer age. It's time you caught up with the times. Don't you know we're about to enter the twenty-first century?''

Rafe wanted to give Shelby Harris a piece of his mind, but not right now. He needed to get something into his empty stomach. He'd missed breakfast that morning, and it was nearly one o'clock.

He opened the door to Maria's and the cool air hit him. After his eyes adjusted to the dim light, he ushered everyone to the table in the corner. He waved to Jill, their waitress.

At first his sister-in-law looked surprised, then a bright smile appeared. She called out to him that she would be right over, then disappeared into the kitchen. He wasn't surprised when she returned with his mother and his grandmother. All three Covelli women made their way to the table.

His mother was tiny and still beautiful with her sparkling brown eyes and short gray hair. Nonna Vittoria was also small in build, but not quite so lively. Her shoulders were slumped, as if she carried the weight of the world on them. But her seventy-plus years hadn't put an end to the quickness of her mind.

"Ely, it's so good to see you," Maria said cheerfully.

"Hello, Ms. Maria, Ms. Vittoria. Nice to see you again."

His mother turned to the teenager. "And this must be your grandson, Josh. My, you have grown into a fine-looking young man."

"Thank you, ma'am. I'll be a senior this year."

Finally Maria turned to her son and placed a kiss on his cheek. "You didn't stop by for breakfast this morning."

"Sorry, Mom," he said. "I was running late."

"You're forgiven. Just introduce me to your friend."

"Mom, Nonna, Jill, this is Shelby Harris. She bought the Stewart place, where we're doing the facade restoration.

Ely and Josh are helping her with some landscape work. We decided to come in for lunch and introduce Shelby around.''

Vittoria stepped forward and touched Shelby's cheek. "So pretty. Are you from around here?"

Shelby shook her head. "No, Louisville."

"Ah, no family from here. But you look familiar. Your green eyes, so *bonita.*" Nonna turned to her grandson and smiled. "Isn't she, Rafaele?"

Rafe bit back a groan. "Yes, Nonna. Now, we'd better eat so I can get back to work."

"Fine, I'll bring the lunch special," Maria said. She and Vittoria bustled back to the kitchen.

"Your family is very nice," Shelby said.

"You sound surprised. What did you expect?"

Shelby took a bread stick from the glass container on the table. "I just meant that you're very lucky."

Shelby didn't think she would ever be able to eat again.

The ravioli had been wonderful, plus, Mrs. Covelli had insisted she take some home, along with her homemade bread.

Back at the house, she put the food in the refrigerator and decided to try to get some work done. But she couldn't concentrate on anything.

Thunder sounded in the distance, and she glanced out the window to see that the wind had picked up and the sky had darkened. It was going to storm. Feeling the sudden drop in temperature, she rubbed her bare arms. She'd sent Ely and Josh home. And the crew from Covelli's had also gone. For some reason, she was restless. More thunder rumbled, alerting her that the front was moving through. She went from room to room, checking to see that the windows were shut. She climbed to the second floor and, after cleaning off the window seat in the master suite, sat and watched as the rain poured down and the lightning zigzagged across the gray sky.

Even as a kid, Shelby had liked thunderstorms. Now she only wished her roof was repaired so she could enjoy them without worrying about the ceiling falling in on her!

She got up and walked down the hall to the attic entrance. Maybe she could find the leaks and put a couple of buckets out to catch the water and stop further damage. Besides, she'd never been in the attic and was curious. Opening the raised wood door to the third floor, she flipped on the switch. A single bulb brightened the dusty narrow staircase. A little apprehensive, Shelby avoided the railing and started the climb. Smelling the musty dampness as she made her way up, she arrived into a large open room. She glanced up at the cobwebs laced in the open rafters.

Oh my, this is…spooky, she thought. She jumped at a sharp crack of thunder and saw lightning flash across the small attic window. Undaunted, she walked to the stack of furniture in the middle of the room—the realtor had told her that there were some things left behind. Shelby pulled back one of the blankets and was surprised to find an oak table and chairs, an iron bed frame and several other treasures she could use to decorate the house.

Then she spied a door in the far wall. She walked over and tried to open it, but it was locked. The key must be downstairs with the other house keys. Hearing the rain pounding on the roof, she decided to wait until another day to investigate.

Shelby continued her search for the source of the main leak. Finally she located a puddle. The rain wasn't coming from overhead but from the window. The runoff from the roof was coming in around the frame and running down the wall to the floor. A bucket wouldn't do any good. Maybe some towels stuffed around the window frame would soak up the moisture. Or she could use the blankets.

She pulled one off a table and carried it to the window. Realizing she wasn't quite tall enough, she dragged over a chair and climbed onto it. When she stood on tiptoe to reach the top of the frame, lightning flashed again. This time the lights flickered and went out.

Shelby screamed as she lost her balance and fell off the chair onto the floor. When her weight came down on her ankle, she felt it twist at an odd angle. The pain hit her and she cried out again.

In the dark Shelby tried not to panic, but she was all alone. Then she heard the noise downstairs. Oh, God. Someone was in the house. She cringed when the sound of footsteps came closer. Her heart pounded, until she heard her name called out.

"Shelby? You up there?" It was Rafe Covelli. She sighed in relief.

"Rafe. I'm here."

A beam from a flashlight illuminated the steps, and then he came into view. "Where are you?"

She could hear the concern in his voice. "Over here."

He hurried across the room and knelt beside her. He looked relieved to see her, then he grinned. "Well, Ms. Harris, seems you need my help once again. What are you going to use to barter yourself out of this one?"

Shelby wanted to punch him in his smug nose, but thought better of it.

"I don't need your help," she insisted as she braced her hand on the chair and tried to stand. She got to her knees then she felt the pain in her ankle and groaned. Automatically Rafe reached out to help, but she shoved his hand away. "I can manage. Just hold the light."

"Sure, you can," he said. "But I'll stand by just in case."

She finally made it to her feet, or at least to one foot.

She didn't dare put any weight on her tender ankle. "See, I'm fine," she said through clenched teeth.

"Okay," he said. "Then we should get downstairs. It isn't safe up here since the storm took out the power."

He stepped back, allowing Shelby to go first. But when she let go of the chair and tried to walk, the pain in her sprained ankle made her cry out.

Rafe dropped the flashlight on the floor and caught her to him. "I've got you," he said hoarsely.

Shelby was pulled against his solid chest, her hands gripping his muscular arms. The comfort of his strength and the soothing sound of his voice was almost intoxicating. He smelled like rain.

But she knew she couldn't continue leaning on him. Experience had taught her that the only person she could depend on was herself. She pushed back, trying to break his hold.

Rafe resisted. "Hey, you can't go it alone, no matter how stubborn you are," he said. He grabbed the flashlight off the floor and handed it to her. Then to her shock, he scooped her up in his arms.

"Put me down," she said, but his grip tightened and her struggles were useless.

"Hush, green eyes," he murmured. "I only want to take you downstairs and check your injury." His dark eyes brimmed with tenderness and compassion.

She felt herself relax, and she nodded. The lightning flashed again. "But…but I'm too heavy."

"You feel fine to me." He smiled. "Now train the flashlight on the stairs, so I can see where I'm going."

Shelby did as he asked and he managed to get her down the narrow steps without further problem. He took her into the master suite and deposited her on the window seat, where light from outside, such as it was, came in. The afternoon sky was still dark gray and the storm showed no sign of letting up.

"Looks like we're in for a wicked night." He knelt down in front of her and started to untie her tennis shoe. "Let's have a look at that ankle."

"I can do it."

He raised his gaze to hers. "Is it me, or do you have trouble letting anyone help you?"

"I don't like to be in anyone's debt," she said, and glanced away from his probing gaze. Every time she'd trusted people, they'd walk out of her life. It was best never to expect anything.

He smiled. "Well, if you plan on staying in Haven Springs, you better get used to people wanting to be neighborly. And maybe if you had asked for help, you wouldn't have had this fall." When his hand gripped her calf, she could feel the heat through her jeans.

"Or are you just a klutz? Does this hurt?" he asked as his fingers gently probed the ankle. His touch was warm against her cool skin.

"Not too much. And I'm not a klutz," she said. "I needed to stop the water. By the way, what were you doing in my house?" she asked.

"I knew the storm was coming, so I stopped by to cover the two-by-fours with some plastic. I saw your car in the driveway and knocked to see if you were okay. When you didn't answer, I came inside and called out. I had a feeling you might be in trouble."

"Because I'm a klutz?"

He smiled and her heart went flip-flop. "No. My dad taught me to help when I can. Someday it might be me in need. I'm not trying to take anything away from you, Shelby. I was just being friendly. I'd say your first week in Haven Springs has been pretty eventful."

More than she wanted. "Thank you...for stopping by." She hated the necessity of expressing gratitude, especially to this man.

He stood. "No problem. I'm going to carry you downstairs and put some ice on this ankle to stop the swelling, so don't go crazy on me."

She couldn't fight him anymore. "Okay."

Rafe put his arms around her back and under her legs, then lifted her into his arms. Having no choice, Shelby put her arms around his neck, drawing them even closer together. He carried her with ease, and when they reached the stairs, he gazed into her eyes.

"Hang on, this'll be a little tricky."

She nodded.

Rafe could feel her breath against his cheek, the warmth of her body against his. The lightning flashed again and he could see the intense look in her eyes. Her dark lashes swept downward, concealing her reaction to his nearness. He didn't know what he was doing to her, but he sure as hell felt what her shapely body was doing to him.

He started down, careful to avoid the weakened steps. Finally they made it to the main floor, and he strode into the front room, where he sat her down on the sofa. "There, safe and sound."

"Thank you," she said. If she didn't watch out, gratitude could get to be a habit.

"I'll go and get some ice cubes out of the freezer." Rafe hurried out of the room and into the kitchen. He went to the old refrigerator and pulled open the door to allow the cool air to bring down the temperature of his body. Finally he pulled out a tray and popped the cubes into a plastic bag he found on the counter. He grabbed a dish towel, then went to the back door and stuck his head out to see if the storm had let up at all.

Damn. Why, for once, did the weatherman have to be right? This storm was supposed to bring heavy rain all evening. He was going to have to stay with Shelby. She couldn't be left alone with a twisted ankle. His thoughts turned to the tempting woman on the sofa.

Just stay away from her, he told himself as he searched

the kitchen drawers for some candles, then started back into the living room. That would be a cinch. Shelby Harris didn't want any part of him. She was too stubborn and independent to ask for help. Rafe wondered what her problem was. Several times he'd caught a truly vulnerable look in her eyes.

He went into the living room and lit the candles, placing them on the end tables, then he put the ice on her swollen ankle.

She winced.

"Do you want me to take you to the clinic?"

"No!" she gasped. "It's just a little tender. By tomorrow it'll be fine."

"If it's the money, I can—"

"I have money," she said defensively.

He was doubtful she had much. It was Shelby Harris's pride that was speaking now.

"I couldn't have bought this house without having some money. In fact, I put a huge amount down. Just about everything I've saved the past ten years. That's the reason I'm a little short on cash at the moment. But I assure you, I make a good living. I'm a graphic artist. I have my own business and several regular clients. Before I went out on my own, I worked for Howell Graphic Design in Louisville." She raised an eyebrow. "Anything else you want to know?"

Rafe was feeling a little ashamed. "I'm sorry. It's none of my business." He looked around the room. "It just seems like you've taken on...a lot."

"Doesn't every new home owner?"

"Yeah, you're right." He sat down on the other end of the sofa and lifted her small foot onto his thigh. "Your ankle needs to be elevated," he said, and couldn't seem to take his hand away from her delicate arch. "I know what it's like to come up a little short. It was only a few months ago that our business was close to going under. After my dad's death we lost a lot of bids. I even had to lay off most of our workers."

"I'm sorry about your father."

"Thanks."

"I take it everything is fine now."

"We're coming back. I wish I could say that I did it on my own, but my brother, Rick, returned home from Texas and put some money into the business. I guess you could say he saved my butt. Then our cousin Tony talked us into expanding beyond carpentry. So we bought some old store-fronts downtown and remodeled the first floors for office space, and the upstairs for low-income apartments to use as a tax break. They're just about ready to rent." He glanced down at her foot. It was so easy and pleasant sitting here with her. "And with the renovations we're doing in the historical district, we're keeping busy. We're hoping to get the bid on the Grand Haven Hotel."

"I bet you will. All I've heard is wonderful things about Covelli and Sons."

Pride swelled his chest. "My father was a master carpenter. He was the one who expanded the business and went after bigger jobs—strip malls and apartment buildings. In fact, he was the project manager for a mall when the accident happened. The investigators said it was his fault, that he'd been using substandard materials and…taking kickbacks." The words stuck in Rafe's throat.

"I don't believe that," Shelby said.

Rafe looked at her. Nightfall had dimmed the room considerably, but he could see the compassion in her eyes. His throat constricted. "How can you be so sure? A lot of his friends believed the worst."

She thrust her hand through her short hair. "I've met you and most of your family. Your principles show, Rafe. I believe you get them from your father." She smiled. "And there're a lot of people in this town who believe in your father's innocence, too. Sometimes we're blamed for things we have no control over."

Rafe saw her glance away, and something told him she was talking from experience. "Nonna Vittoria blames it all on the curse."

"The what?"

Rafe smiled. "The Covelli curse." He gave Shelby a quick rundown of the story about his grandparents.

Shelby tried to listen intently and at the same time ignore the unbelievable sensations he was causing just by touching her foot. "Do you believe in the curse?"

He shrugged. "Sometimes, but the important thing is Nonna believes in it and she blames herself. According to her, everything bad that happens to our family is because of the curse, including the fact that I'm not married."

"Do you think that's the reason?"

Rafe's eyes raised to hers. His dark good looks were mesmerizing. She suspected he could have any woman he wanted.

"In the past I haven't wanted to. There's Nonna, Mom and my sister, Angelina, to take care of. Another woman would have been one too many."

Shelby held back her laughter. After hearing about Maria Covelli, a successful businesswoman, Shelby doubted that his mother needed much help from her sons. "From what I've heard of the women in your family, they seem capable of taking care of themselves."

"Oh, I catch your drift. Another woman who can get along just fine without a man."

"I didn't say that. I meant that they can support themselves. We aren't always the weaker sex."

"Then there is only one thing to do. Put your money where your mouth is."

"What do you mean?" She thought she saw a glint of humor in his eyes.

He stood, careful not to hurt her ankle. "I'll be here

Saturday afternoon and we'll start tearing out the ceiling in the front bedroom. You're my new helper. As long as your ankle is healed, that is.''

"But you said…"

"What's the matter, Shelby? Afraid you can't keep up?" She shook her head. "I can't pay, so I can't accept."

"What? Accept help from a friend even when he's going to put you to work? Dammit, you are the most stubborn woman I have ever met."

"I'm not any stubborner than you are," she argued. Shelby managed to work her way up to stand on one foot— and teetered right into Rafe's arms.

He caught her easily. She looked up and their eyes locked.

"If you're as smart as I think you are, green eyes, you better send me home."

"I don't need you anymore, Rafe, so go home," she said breathlessly.

He didn't move for the longest time. Then he gently cupped her face, his long fingers tracing her cheek. "You're a liar, Shelby Harris," he whispered huskily as his thumb moved to her bottom lip. Her heart pounded against the incredible sensation his action produced.

"You're a beautiful woman, Shelby, and hard to resist," he murmured, then lowered his head to hers. "Too hard." His mouth closed over hers in a heated kiss.

Shelby couldn't find the strength to protest, nor did she want to. The feelings Rafe Covelli created in her were like nothing she'd ever experienced before. All too soon he broke off the kiss.

He stepped back, looking at her intensely. "I think we need to set new guidelines if we're going to work together."

Chapter Four

Thirty minutes later Rafe walked through the back door and into the kitchen of the Covelli house. The electricity had come back on and there didn't seem to be any damage from the rain. Outside there were branches down along the streets, but Haven Springs had survived the severe summer storm.

But would he?

He pulled out a chair and sat down. Hell, what was he doing kissing Shelby Harris? He had no business... He rubbed his eyes, then ran his hands over his face, hoping to erase the unbelievable feelings she caused in him. He could still smell her fresh scent, and feel the way she fit against his body. It had been so long since he'd held a woman...kissed...wanted...

A stirring began deep inside. He ignored it. Hell, no wonder she'd kicked him out, insisting she could take care of herself.

He crossed to the refrigerator, pulled out some leftover spaghetti, then put it in the microwave.

He turned around and discovered that Rick had come in. "Hi, bro."

"Hi, Rick."

"Quite a storm we had." Rick went to the refrigerator, took out a beer and popped the top. "Where have you been all evening?"

"Since when do I have to report to you?"

"Whoa. Just making conversation." Rick raised his hands. "Mom was worried."

"Sorry." Rafe released a long breath. "I went over to the Stewart place to cover the wood I had delivered this morning."

"Took you three hours?"

Rafe glared at his brother. "It shouldn't have, but when the storm blew out the power, I went inside to see if Shelby was okay. I couldn't find her. Then I heard a scream from up in the attic. She was trying to plug a leak in the roof. She'd fallen off a chair and hurt her ankle."

Rick raised an eyebrow. "She all right?"

"I took her downstairs and got her some ice."

His brother smiled knowingly. "So you had to care for her injuries."

Rafe nodded. "Yeah, but she was prickly as hell about it."

"A woman with fire to match her auburn hair," Rick said with a big grin. "Interesting."

"Nothing interesting about it. I'm just trying to figure out a way to make working there pay off. Financially," he added quickly.

"You spent several hours with a pretty woman and all you thought about was work? I take it you don't care for those long legs."

Rafe tensed. He didn't like his brother noticing Shelby's attributes. "Hey, you're a married man. What are you doing looking at another woman's legs?"

"I've got eyes." His brother grinned. "My, aren't we defensive about someone we've barely noticed."

Rafe had noticed all right. He noticed how good she felt in his arms. How her kiss turned him inside out. But he had no right to these feelings. There was no room in his life for a woman, no matter how badly he wanted her.

"I'm only defensive because you're wrong about the situation. I've got a job to do and Shelby Harris is causing a lot of distractions…I mean, trouble."

Rick slapped his brother on the back. "Oh, boy, you've got it bad."

Rafe hissed out an impatient breath. "How many times do I have to tell you—"

"—there's nothing between us," Rick finished for his brother. "Look, what's wrong with falling for the woman? Shelby seems nice enough. And she might even be able to put up with you."

"Falling for her? Are you nuts? I don't have time for…a relationship."

"That's crazy," Rick said. "What's so pressing?"

"This family, for one. Mom, Nonna and Angelina, and I still have this mess with Dad."

"We're all helping to solve that. It's time you started to think about a personal life."

Rafe shook his head. "No. I'm no good at the man-woman thing. Remember?"

Rick frowned. "If you're talking about Jeannie, that was years ago. You were both just kids in college."

Rafe didn't know if it was possible to forget how badly Jeannie had hurt him. She'd taken his love and used him. His thoughts turned to Shelby. He had to admit that she nearly had him down for the count with that kiss earlier, but he also knew that even if he opened his heart to her, she might not accept it. So why take the chance?

* * *

By morning the rain had stopped and everything looked beautiful. Shelby awoke early and went outside in the back-yard to have her coffee and toast. Her ankle was a little tender, but the swelling had gone down and she could walk on it.

She sat in an old wooden deck chair she'd dragged out of the shed. The sun felt wonderful, making her think that all was right with the world, that buying this big house hadn't been the dumbest thing she'd ever done. Then her thoughts wandered to Rafe, the same thoughts that had kept her awake half the night. His kiss had stirred up all sorts of feelings in her. And she wasn't happy about it. Just stay away from the man, she told herself. But that would be impossible since she was going to be working with him.

"Mornin', Miss Shelby," Ely called.

"Good morning, Ely." She got up and walked to the rose garden to see the Cullen men, Ely and Josh, already busy working. They had cleared away most of the weeds and dead rosebushes. The ones that still showed signs of life, Ely had trimmed.

"Looks like you've been busy."

Ely tipped back his straw hat. "Guess I'm a little anxious to return things to normal."

"Me, too," she said. After making the older man prom-ise not to overdo it, Shelby left and continued down the path toward the cottage.

She wanted to fix this place up, but like a lot of things, it would have to wait until the house was finished and she began taking in paying guests. She stepped onto the rotting wooden porch and went to the door. She tried several keys the realtor had given her before she found the right one. Pushing open the stubborn door, she crossed the threshold into a large room with a fireplace and kitchenette. The fur-niture was covered with sheets that were filthy with dust.

As Shelby moved farther into the room, her gaze combed the area for anything that was familiar.

She had been only six at the time, but she remembered the wicker sofa and chairs, along with the big flowery pillows she used to lie on to watch television. The ancient portable still sat in the corner. She walked to the kitchenette. In the cabinets, she found the delicate china dishes with the rosebud trim she'd remembered. There was a small maple table in front of the window that looked out toward the big house. This was where she and her mother used to have breakfast on those summer mornings more than twenty years ago.

Shelby continued on to the bedroom, where she found the old double bed with the white headboard and matching dresser. When she was a child, she'd thought this was a princess's house. She'd never wanted to leave. She and her mother had never lived in a place that lovely. It had usually been short stays in one-room apartments. Sometimes they'd had to leave in the middle of the night. Later Shelby realized that was because they didn't have the rent or were running from one of Nola's boyfriends.

But that long-ago summer at Stewart Manor was different. Shelby had felt as if she belonged. There were no men who yelled or pushed her mom around. And she didn't have to go to a baby-sitter because her mom had to work. There were pretty flowers outside the windows, and a nice lady who used to bring her cookies and ice cream. Miss Hannah. Shelby had liked her. She would hug Shelby and say that they could live in the cottage forever.

But that hadn't turned out to be true. Shelby drew a shaky breath, fighting back the raw feelings, remembering the years of loneliness. She had always longed for a home like other kids had. Why had she and her mother had to leave?

She remembered that last day as if it were yesterday.

"Get your things together, Shelby," her mother had said. "We're moving."

Nola Harris pulled out the familiar battered suitcase and began to empty the drawers into it.

"No, Mom. You promised we could stay here for a long time."

"We can't. Now do as I told you."

Panic raced through Shelby as she clutched the doll Miss Hannah had given her the day they'd arrived at the cottage. "But you said I could live in the princess house." Tears slid down her cheeks. "Please, Mommy, I'll be good if you let me stay. I want to stay. Miss Hannah said we could."

Nola looked angry. "Well, Miss Hannah lied. She wants us gone. So we're going. Now for the last time, put your things in the suitcase."

As usual Shelby did as she was told, then she and her mother took the bus out of Haven Springs. They went to Louisville, where her mother soon hooked up with Orin. A short time after that, Shelby ended up in foster care. Even her mom hadn't wanted her anymore....

Shelby brushed away a tear. That was so long ago. For the past twenty-three years she'd managed just fine on her own. She didn't need a mother. Or anyone. But she refused to cheat herself out of a home. And this was the only place she'd ever felt she belonged.

A sudden scratching noise from inside the closet drew Shelby from her thoughts. Her heart began to race as she wondered if it was a rat. She went to the closet door and was about to peek inside when the scratching intensified. No way. She hurried out as quickly as she could with her tender ankle, but before she made it out the door she collided with Rafe.

He smiled. "What's got you moving so fast?"

"There's some kind of animal in the closet," she said, hating herself for being so fearful. "Something big."

"Well, there haven't been any bear sightings in Haven Springs lately."

"Very funny. If you're going to be sarcastic, then you can just leave. I'll handle it myself." She squared her shoulders and started to head back into the bedroom.

"Whoa." He grasped her arm to stop her, his touch warm on her skin. "If it's a squirrel or some other rodent, it might come out fighting." He eyed her shorts appreciatively. "I think I'm better dressed for the job." He was wearing jeans and work boots. Before she could protest, he went into the bedroom.

After a few minutes he called to her. "Come and meet your stowaway."

Shelby walked into the room to find Rafe kneeling down at the closet door. "What is it?" She peered inside and saw a fluffy black-and-white kitten. "Oh, my. It's so cute." The cat mewed pitifully. "How did it get in here?" Shelby knelt beside Rafe and put out her hand so the cat would see she didn't mean any harm.

"From what I can tell, it came in through the missing glass in the window to get out of the rain last night. It must have wandered into the closet and the wind more than likely blew the door shut. Luckily you came here today, or the kitten probably wouldn't have survived long."

Rafe watched Shelby pick up the animal and cuddle it in her arms. He was a little envious at the attention she lavished on the scrawny stray.

"You're lucky we found you, little guy," she crooned.

"Uh, I think he's a girl," Rafe said.

Shelby's smile was unguarded as she continued to fawn over the kitten. Rafe's gaze moved down Shelby's body, remembering last night when he'd held her in his arms. Now her long legs were bared for his viewing. They really *were* beautiful.

"Ouch!" she cried. "She scratched me."

"Let me see." He reached for her hand and found a long red line across her knuckle, but the skin wasn't broken. He looked up and was transfixed by her shimmering green eyes. "She's probably just a little frightened from being trapped. You want me to take her to the pound?" he said, suspecting that was the last thing she'd want.

"You can't take her to the pound! Wouldn't she belong to someone around here?"

"I doubt it. From the looks of her, she hasn't eaten in a while."

Shelby continued stroking the kitten. "I think I should keep her in case someone is looking for her." She met Rafe's eyes. "I mean, I did find her. That makes me responsible for her."

"I rescued you last night—does that mean I'm responsible for you?"

"I didn't need rescuing," she said, standing. "I could have gotten downstairs by myself."

Her stubbornness amused him. "If you say so."

Her eyes flashed. "I say so." She hugged the cat to her chest. "But thanks for your help."

He watched her walk away and suddenly remembered why he'd been looking for her. "Shelby, how's your ankle this morning?"

"It's fine. Practically good as new."

"I'm glad," he said, figuring she'd rather be tortured than admit she was hurt and have to ask for help. "I also wanted to ask you if it's okay to go up into the attic today. I have time this afternoon to start patching the roof. If we have three days of clear weather, I could probably get the job done by then." His eyes locked onto her mouth and he found himself thinking about the kiss they shared. The sweet taste...the softness of her lips...

Shelby felt Rafe's piercing gaze. Was he thinking about their kiss, or had he forgotten about it already? After all, he'd probably kissed a lot of women. "I'm going to pay you, so make sure I get a bill."

He stood there for a long time just looking at her.

"Is there something wrong?" she asked.

"About last night... I was out of line. I never should have kissed you." His sexy, intense eyes never wavered from hers.

"Right," she managed to say.

He nodded. "If you're worried about it happening again—"

"I'm not," she interrupted, "because I won't let it."

Again he nodded. "You have my promise that I'll stay away from you. I don't want you to be afraid that I'll make a pass every time I get close to you."

She forced a laugh. "Look, I know I'm not irresistible—you made that perfectly clear. Forget about it." She pushed past him and went as fast as her ankle would allow toward the house, hearing him call after her. But she'd already shut out the hurt and rejection, just as she had all those times as a child.

About one o'clock Rafe took a plastic pan along with cat litter and a few assorted necessities for Lucky—the name Shelby had bestowed on the kitten—out of the back of his truck. He grabbed the pizza box from the front seat, kicked the door shut with his foot, then headed up the back steps. Why was he doing this? He must be crazy. He was supposed to stay clear of Shelby Harris. Instead, he'd bought toys and food for her mangy cat. He knocked and waited nervously for an answer.

The door opened and Shelby appeared.

He held out the box. "Thought you might be in need of some cat supplies."

She took the pan. "Oh, thank you, but you didn't have to—"

"I know." He decided he liked her short hair. "And I stopped by Mom's and she insisted I bring you this pizza." He saw her eyes light up when he walked past her and set everything on the counter.

"Thank you. I'll pay you back."

"You know, Shelby, not all people do things to get paid back. They do them just for the sake of being kind. Well, I better get back to work." He started to saunter off.

"Wait, Rafe," she called after him. "Have you eaten?"

He stopped at the door. "No, I've been too busy."

"Would you like to share some of this?"

He smiled. "I'd love to, ma'am."

"Stop calling me that." She went to the refrigerator and took out a pitcher of iced tea.

"I thought all you Southern gals liked that."

"Louisville is only fifty miles from here," she said as Lucky wandered into the room.

Rafe reached into the plastic pan, pulled out a small ball and tossed it on the floor for the kitten to play with. Lucky took off after it. "Is that where your parents live, too?"

Shelby looked away. "No. My parents are…gone."

"I'm sorry." She carried two glasses of tea to the counter. "It was a long time ago. I've been on my own for a while."

Rafe shook his head. "It doesn't matter. I still miss my dad a lot. There are times when I want to ask his advice, then realize that I have to figure things out on my own."

Shelby sat down on a stool and studied the sadness in Rafe's eyes. Did he realize how lucky he was to have had all those years with a father?

He shook his head. "Sorry. Didn't mean to get all maudlin on you."

"No, that's all right. You loved your father. It's only natural to feel these things…to miss him." Shelby had no idea where or even who her father was. As a little girl she dreamed he'd come for her someday, tell her how much he wanted her in his life. Then she grew up and realized that was never going to happen.

"I'll feel better when we get this mess with his accident straightened out." Rafe grimaced. "I should have been the one who went to the site and checked..." He glanced away, as if he realized he'd said too much, then opened the pizza box and offered her the first slice.

She took a bite and sighed in pleasure. "Oh, this is so good!"

She had another bite and got sauce on her lips. She used her tongue to clean it away and caught Rafe watching her. She felt herself blush.

Rafe cleared his throat, but it didn't clear his mind of the wicked thought he was having about Shelby. "Didn't I tell you?"

"This is the best pizza I've ever tasted." She took another bite. Again Rafe stared at her. She seemed to take such pleasure in eating—her face was so expressive. He wasn't thinking about devouring pizza.

"I may have to splurge and have two slices."

"Go crazy," he urged.

With the distractions, Rafe only managed to eat three slices. They did a little polite talking, almost too polite, but he wasn't going to push it. Something had happened to her in the cottage this morning. Something besides finding a kitten. Maybe, in time, she would trust him enough to tell him about it.

"Well, I better get back to work so I won't set a bad example for the crew. I'm going to fix those stairs. Then I need to get up on the roof."

"I'll be working in the front room if you need me," she said.

Rafe found he needed her—badly. And it had nothing to

do with working on the house. He stood. "I'll be fine. I'm taking Doug Peters up with me. He's a roofer."

"What's that going to cost?"

"Nothing. He owes me a favor."

Shelby could not help but stare at the powerfully built man in front of her. The way his T-shirt hugged his broad chest and muscular arms made a woman want to lean on him. There was a deep longing in her stomach. "What do you do? Go around and help out the whole town?"

Rafe grinned that slow, sexy grin. "Just my friends. Thanks for lunch, green eyes." He turned and left the room.

Shelby watched the man until he disappeared, thinking it was a bad idea to let him get too close. In her years in foster care, she'd learned to always watch her back. Everyone wanted something, especially men. She learned that from seeing her mother's life being destroyed.

She tossed the box in the trash, went into the living room and sat down at the computer. She had finished all her artwork this morning. It was ready to go to the post office. That left her a little time to work on her story.

Three years ago Shelby had started writing about her make-believe childhood friend Kellie Anne. Then on a whim, she'd sent the story of the five-year-old girl's adventures to a publisher. To her surprise, they bought the first story and two more after that. The fourth book was due at the end of the month. Kellie Anne had become popular as the paperback books found their way into homes and schools.

Each book had been a fantasy of Shelby's when she'd been a child and alone and afraid. She would dream up a safe place and take along her friend, Kellie Anne. Shelby hadn't gotten rich so far, but she enjoyed writing the books, and her next month's royalty check was going to help pay for the repairs she needed on her house.

Then she could open her bed-and-breakfast and fill it with *real* people.

By late afternoon, Rafe had finished the repairs to the stairs, using enough wood to replace the broken steps and to make the staircase safe. He and Shelby could decide how to finish the job later.

Next he'd gone up on the roof with Doug. For two hours in the hottest part of the day, they'd replaced roofing tiles. And the job wasn't done yet; he would be back tomorrow afternoon. He only hoped that Shelby appreciated his efforts.

He pulled the truck into the office parking lot and went inside to find his sister Angelina at her desk. He smiled at the pretty brunette. "What's up?"

"Nothing. But looks like you've been busy." She studied his sweat-soaked shirt and filthy jeans.

"Unlike some of us who have cushy jobs, I've been working."

"I work," she protested.

"You push buttons on a computer."

Angelina smiled and she looked as beautiful as their mother. She was also smart as a whip—but totally focused on a career. Rafe hated the fact that after losing her college sweetheart, Justin Hinshaw, to leukemia, she'd refused to allow another man into her life.

"It's more than you can do on a computer."

"I could if I wanted to," he said. "I just need to learn."

"Oh, no you don't." She held up her hands. "I've been through that and I refuse to do it again."

"What if I don't need you to teach me. What if someone else is willing?"

"More power to them. I'm just glad..." She paused and narrowed her eyes. "Wait a minute. Who's going to teach you? You refused to take a class. And why are you suddenly so eager to learn, anyway? Didn't you threaten to toss out my computer?''

''That's because you don't have long legs like Shelby Harris.''

Two heads turned to find Rick standing in the doorway. ''So you're going to let Ms. Harris show you a thing or two,'' he said.

Rafe hated his brother's knowing look. Wasn't anything private around here? ''She offered to show me some things.''

''Ooh, this is getting interesting.'' Angelina leaned back in her chair. ''I hear our newest resident is tall and pretty.''

Rafe ignored his sister and picked up his stack of phone messages. ''You could say that.''

''Mom and Nonna said she's beautiful.'' Angelina turned to Rick. ''Is she?''

Rick nodded. ''She's not as pretty as Jill, of course, but she's not hard on the eyes.''

''Are you going to ask her out, Rafe?'' Angelina asked.

''She's a client,'' he snapped.

Rick crossed the room. ''She's also the only woman you've shown any interest in for years. But are you ready to take on the Covelli curse?''

Chapter Five

The following Monday morning, Rafe sat in on a meeting at the office with Rick, Angelina and Tony. They were listening to Billy Jacobs, the private investigator who had been looking into their dad's accident.

"So you're saying that Adam Kirby just looked the other way and allowed substandard lumber to leave the Hardin Lumberyard?" Rafe asked.

Billy was in his middle forties. The good old Texas boy was dressed in jeans and a Western-cut white shirt. He shook his head. "Not at first," he began. "Adam questioned the owner's son, Pete Hardin, but he told him not to worry about it, said they were using a new mill. But Adam suspected there was more going on, since stacks of wood were covered and only certain men were asked to move them."

"Why didn't Adam just go to Pete's father?" Rick asked.

Billy frowned. "From what Adam told me, Peter, Sr. was in rough shape. His heart attack had been pretty bad, and besides, he believed his boy was honest and could run the business on his own.''

"Hell, the building code in that area specifies grade-one lumber on all two-story structures,'' Rafe said. "I was there with Dad when he talked with the building engineer and when he wrote the order.''

"Did your father suspect anything?''

Rafe nodded. "Yeah, there was a call from one of the framers, so Dad headed out to the site to have a look.''

No one needed to go over the facts of the accident that had injured one crew member and killed Rafaele, Sr. When the second story gave way, their dad was crushed. Rafe winced. Like his dad, he knew that something was going on. He should have been the one who'd gone out to see about it. Not Dad. Rafe was going to pay for that mistake for the rest of his life. Now Pete Hardin, Jr. was going to pay, too.

Rafe made a fist. "I want to get that SOB.''

"So do I, but we're going to do it all nice and legally,'' Billy said calmly. "That's the only way it'll hold up in court.''

Rick came up beside his brother. "We'll get him, bro. We'll get the creep who did this. Then Dad'll be at peace.''

"Damn. I want to bring him down, Rick,'' Rafe said through a clenched jaw. "He just as good as killed our father.''

"Drugs do strange things to a person,'' Billy said. "And from what I found out, Pete Hardin is pretty heavy into cocaine. I expect he was spending hundreds of dollars a day.''

"Drugs are no excuse. What he did was criminal. I want him put away—for good.''

"Dad wouldn't want revenge,'' Angelina said. "But he would want to know this guy couldn't hurt anyone else. That'll be true justice.''

"The main thing we want is for everyone to know that Rafaele Covelli would never compromise his principles," said Tony. He had been like another son to Rafaele, Sr. He'd lived with the family since college and had been their financial adviser for the past five years.

Billy smiled. "I wish I could have known Rafaele, Sr. He sounds like a hell of a guy. I know he'd be awfully proud of his kids."

Later that night Rafe sat at the bar in the restaurant. He was glad the place was quiet because he wasn't fit company.

He knew he had to be patient to wait for Billy to gather the evidence necessary to have Hardin arrested, but Rafe didn't like waiting for anything. He'd been waiting two years too long already.

"How you doing?"

Rafe looked up to find Jill on the other side of the bar. "Looks like you could use this." She handed him a beer. "I hear it was a pretty rough meeting today," she said.

"Thanks. How did you know?" He raised the bottle and took a long pull.

"Rick came home just before I left for my shift. Although he'd never admit it, I know it was hard on him, too. I'm going to get off early and take him some of your mom's lasagna. That should cheer him up."

"That and you being there for him." Knowing his brother had Jill to comfort him made Rafe realize how lonely he was.

"Hey, don't look now, but there's a tall brunette looking this way."

Rafe glanced over his shoulder to see Shelby standing by the door. "I bet she's here to pick up her order," Jill said, and walked toward Shelby.

Rafe wanted to call her back, knowing his sister-in-law

would do nothing short of dragging Shelby over to him. He glanced at her pretty face. She wasn't exactly beautiful, but her features were...dazzling, with her huge green eyes, her perky nose and full lips.

Shelby's gaze met his and her shy smile appeared. Suddenly he brightened and smiled back.

It wasn't long before Jill took Shelby's hand and pulled her over to the bar. "Look who's here, Rafe. Shelby."

"Hi, Shelby." His heart was racing as he took in her face and figure. She wore new-looking jeans and a white blouse.

She nervously tucked her hair behind her ears. "Hi, Rafe."

"Back for more of Mom's cooking?"

"Yeah, you got me hooked," she admitted. "Thought I'd try the lasagna tonight."

"Shelby's eating all alone tonight," Jill said. "I told her she should stay here and share a meal with...friends." Just then Maria and Angelina came out of the kitchen. Jill went to greet them.

Rafe groaned. "You'll never get out of here now."

Shelby's eyes widened. "Why?"

"Because Jill has got reinforcements. Don't worry, I'll help you escape. Just follow my lead."

Maria was the first to hug Shelby. "Shelby, it's so good to see you. I don't believe you've met my daughter, Angelina. Angelina, this is Shelby Harris. She bought Stewart Manor."

Angelina smiled. "So nice to finally meet you." She glanced at Rafe. "My brother here has been keeping you to himself."

Shelby blushed. "Not really—I've been so busy with the house and keeping up with my work that I haven't gone out much."

"Shelby runs her own business," Rafe volunteered. "She's a graphic artist."

Angelina's blue eyes lit up. "An independent woman. How interesting. And now you're going to turn the Stewart house into a bed-and-breakfast."

Shelby glanced at Rafe. "There's still a lot to do before that happens. In fact, I have to go slower than I first thought. The repairs are expensive."

Angelina smiled. "Maybe you and Rafe can work something out." She winked at her brother.

Rafe looked at Shelby, who seemed to be enjoying herself. Then he saw the gleam in his mother's eyes, then his sister's. He knew they were matchmaking.

Just then a busboy arrived with a white container for Shelby.

"Well, I'd better get home," Shelby said. "Nice meeting you, Angelina. Maria."

"You sure you don't want to eat here?" Maria asked.

"Maybe another time."

Rafe took Shelby by the arm. "Shelby has a deadline. And with the noise of the work crew during the daytime, the evenings are all she has." He guided her toward the door and whispered in her ear, "Just follow me." He looked back at the group of women who managed to track them to the door. "And Shelby has been having trouble with her car, so I'm going to follow her to make sure she gets home."

The trio smiled. "That so nice of you," Maria said.

"Just doing what Dad taught me," he said, and pushed Shelby out the door into the balmy summer night. "Keep walking to the curb."

"I don't need you to follow me home," Shelby said.

"You do if you don't want the Covelli family to insist you stay here and answer questions all night." He opened the door to her compact car and looked at her as the moonlight created an intimate glow around her. He'd been wrong. She was beautiful. "Please get in. I'm not in the mood to deal with my family right now."

She finally relented and got in her car. Then he went to his truck. After she pulled away from the curb, he did the same and tossed a quick wave to the three smiling women in the restaurant window.

Shelby pulled into her driveway and got out with her dinner. Rafe's truck pulled in behind her and she walked over to him.

"I made it home okay."

"Sure you don't want me to check for any *big* wild animal before I leave?" He smiled and she found she wasn't as immune to this good-looking man as she'd hoped.

"Careful or I'll set Lucky on you."

"Ohh, I'm real afraid," he teased.

Shelby stood next to his truck like a teenager talking to her boyfriend. "Okay, you big strong man, I know you're never afraid of anything."

He sobered. "You might be surprised. We all have our moments."

Her smile died when she saw the vulnerability in his dark eyes. She had a feeling he didn't want to be alone tonight, and she had to admit that she didn't, either. She held up her container. "I know it's not much, but would you like to share my dinner? I was going to add a salad and maybe a bottle of wine that a neighbor, Mrs. Kerrigan, brought over in a welcome basket."

"I thought you were going to work tonight."

"I can do that anytime." She hated this business of being neighborly. She wasn't very good at it. "But it's okay— I'll understand if you don't want to stay. Night, Rafe." She started for the door, then she heard him shut off the engine and slam the truck door. He caught up with her at the porch.

"You know, my family comes from Tuscany, Italy. Wine country. We're purists. I can't drink anything that doesn't come in a corked bottle."

She laughed. "So I take it you're staying."

"I'm suddenly starving." He draped his arm across her shoulders.

The closeness should have bothered her, but she realized that it was just part of Rafe's personality. He was a touchy-feely kind of person. His entire family was. She unlocked the back door, walked inside and turned on the kitchen light. Lucky was there to greet them.

"Well, how you doing, little one?" Rafe picked her up and cuddled her in his large arms. Lucky purred noisily. Shelby felt a sudden emptiness inside, but quickly pushed it away and went to the refrigerator for the salad fixings.

After putting down the cat, Rafe washed his hands and picked up the bottle of wine from the basket. Shelby didn't have a corkscrew, but the pocket knife Rafe carried came with one. Soon he had the wine open and poured into glasses.

He took a sip. "Hey, this isn't bad."

"Mrs. Kerrigan said it's from a vineyard in Texas. Her sister, Esther, is visiting and brought a few bottles with her."

"She visits every year about this time. Rose Kerrigan has been trying to get her to move up here for years. Both are widowed and live alone."

"You know a lot of people in town."

"I grew up here. Never lived anywhere else. And in the carpentry business you get to know people." He leaned against the counter. "Don't you know a lot of people in Louisville?"

"Not really. I moved around a lot as a kid."

"Your dad military or something?"

"Or something." She turned away and finished the salads. The last thing she wanted to discuss was her family. "Your family is nice." She glanced over her shoulder to see his smile.

"Mom and Nonna mean well," he said, "but they believe that the only happy man is a married man. When Rick returned last year and took a liking to Jill, they went crazy. I hate to say this, but they're playing matchmakers again. You just have to hang tough. After a while they leave you alone."

"Why would they single me out? They don't even know me."

"It's a feeling about you, my *nonna* says. You have a good heart. Your honesty shines through your eyes."

Shelby was shocked at his words. "I've only met her once."

He shrugged. "That doesn't matter."

Shelby needed to change the subject. "I like your sister. Does she work in the business, too?"

Rafe sipped his wine. "Angelina graduated from college two years ago. I'm not sure that working in a construction office is what she wants, but she helped keep things together for me. I think she wants to get established in her career. I'm a little reluctant to let her go. She's so young. And there are so many jerks out there."

Shelby set the salad bowls on a tray and took down two plates from the cupboard, along with some flatware. She dished out the lasagna. "Let's go into the other room."

Rafe grabbed the wine with the glasses and followed her into the dining room, where there was a large trestle table with eight matching chairs.

He walked around the table, his hands caressing the polished oak. "Where did this come from?"

"I found it in the attic the other night. I paid Josh and two of his friends to carry it downstairs." She ran her hand over the smooth finish. "I know I should have waited until you're finished with the work, but I couldn't resist."

"It's a beautiful set. Why wasn't it auctioned with the other things?"

"I'm not sure, but the realtor said I'm welcome to anything that was left behind."

"Well, you got a gem of a deal here." He looked closer. "When we start to sand the floors, we'll cover it up. It should be okay."

She set two place mats down on the table and arranged the plates, then Rafe pulled out her chair. "I can't wait until I have guests to fill up these chairs."

Rafe took a seat at the head of the table. There wasn't any lack of dinner conversation. Rafe talked about his life in Haven Springs, his family coming from Italy after the Second World War.

He poured them some more wine. Something Shelby didn't need. The Covellis were probably raised on the stuff. Not her. But she found that she liked the relaxed feeling the drink gave her and how easy Rafe was to talk to.

"I've told you about my dad's death in an accident at a work site. Today we discovered that the person who sold him inferior materials was a guy who needed the money so he could buy drugs to support his habit." He stood and walked to the window. "A man is dead because of someone's selfishness. And this guy is walking around free."

Shelby got up and went to him. She had no idea what to do. She wanted to reach out, but would he repel her offer? Taking the chance, she raised her hand to touch his back. He stiffened, then slowly began to relax.

"I have to fight to keep from going out and killing this guy." He turned around with his fist clenched, and Shelby jumped back.

Rafe saw fear in her eyes and hated himself for causing

it. "Shelby, I'm sorry. I didn't mean to frighten you. I wasn't going to hit you. I'd never hit a woman."

"I know that," she said. "You just caught me off guard."

She walked away. But he could tell she was still shaken. *What man did this to you?* he wondered. Picking up the glasses of wine, he followed her into the front room.

A small, dim lamp was turned on by her computer. He went to the machine and watched as colorful squiggly lines danced across the screen. He saw the CD player and he reached out and pressed for disk number one. Soon the soft sounds of Michael Bolton filled the air. He turned to Shelby.

"Here, drink this," he said. "It'll help you relax."

"If I get any more relaxed, I'll fall asleep."

"Is that a hint for me to go?" His eyes met hers and he found he didn't want to leave.

She shrugged. "If you have someplace you need to go…"

"I'm where I want to be, but it would be nice if you asked me to stay." He stepped closer. "Is that so hard, Shelby? To ask?"

He watched her swallow, then his gaze moved to the pulse fluttering in her neck. Her long, graceful neck.

"You're welcome to stay—awhile."

He put the wine down on the table, freeing his hands. Then he reached out and cupped the back of her neck. Her eyes widened. "Oh, green eyes, do you realize how badly I want to stay? How badly I need you to hold to make me forget this hellish day?"

Her breathing grew labored. Her gaze danced over his face. She was feeling everything he was feeling. Yet he knew that if he took her in his arms, he'd never want to let her go. But that didn't stop his hunger for her, his desire to feel her body against his.

He pulled her to his chest, and his mouth closed over hers. Heat ignited between them. He tasted her with his tongue, delving to find her secrets, but that only succeeded in making him want more. He tightened his hold on her, his hands moving up and down her back, feeling every curve, aching to make love to her. But one night wouldn't be enough. A warning signal went off and he broke the kiss.

His forehead leaned against hers as he tried to catch his breath. "Oh, *cara,* you could make a man forget his name."

He pulled back and touched her swollen mouth with his finger. "If things were different... If I could..."

She stiffened and pulled away. "Don't, Rafe. Don't make this more than it is. We had dinner together to ward off the loneliness. Then we shared a kiss. A simple kiss. I don't believe in promises. They're just float-away words, words that never mean anything."

What she said was like a blow to the gut, and he hadn't expected it. "Well, I guess it's time I head home. Thanks for the dinner and the...nice kiss." He turned and walked out the door. He could give her another sample of a nice kiss that would blow her socks off, but why try? At least this way he could save a little of his pride. He stepped out into the night air.

Pride was about all she'd left him.

Rafe spent the next hour driving around. He went out to Patoka Lake and then back through town. He stopped at the park, then took off around town again. Somehow he ended up at Rick's house. It was well after midnight, and the place was dark, but that didn't stop him from knocking on the door.

Finally Rick opened the door. He was dressed in a pair

of jeans and nothing else. "Rafe, what are you doing here? Is something the matter? Is Nonna or Mom sick?"

Rafe held up his hand. "No, Rick, they're all fine. It's me."

His brother looked over his shoulder as if expecting someone to appear behind him. "What's wrong with you?"

"I got a problem—"

"Honey, who is it?" Jill called, then showed up at the door in a silky nightgown and robe. These two didn't look like they'd been sleeping at all. Great, he'd interrupted their lovemaking. Ah, hell, he was blowing everything tonight.

"Look, I shouldn't have disturbed you," Rafe said. "I'm sorry, Jill. Bro, I'll talk to you tomorrow." He turned to leave, but Rick grabbed his arm.

"You aren't going anywhere, Rafe. Sit on the step and cool off a minute," he ordered. "I'll be right back."

Rafe nodded and did what he was told. He sank down on the top step of the old house and watched as the lightning bugs danced in front of him. A few minutes later, Rick returned with two beers, handed him one, then took a seat beside him. "You look like you need this."

Rafe tipped back his head and swallowed. Then he frowned into the darkness. "You remember when we used to run around the yard and try to catch lightning bugs and put them in a jar?"

"Quit stalling, Rafe. Something has to be important for you to show up on my doorstep in the middle of the night."

"Okay, okay." He held up his hand. "I need to ask you something."

"Go ahead."

"Were you really sure about Jill from the beginning, or did you fight it?"

"I fought it like hell. I wanted her, but I thought that she could do much better with someone else, someone who would be better at sticking around."

"What made you change your mind?"

Rick cocked an eyebrow.

"Is this questioning going somewhere?"

"Yeah. Just tell me."

"Okay, I realized that if I didn't stand by Jill, someone else would, someone else would be kissing her, making love to her, sharing her and Lucas's lives. I couldn't stand that thought. That's when I knew I really loved her."

Rafe groaned. "Okay, now you can say, I told you so."

"What are you talking about?"

"It's Shelby."

Rick smiled slowly. "Got it bad, do ya?"

"I wish I didn't, but no matter what, she keeps getting closer and closer."

"Then what the hell are you doing here? You should be with her."

Rafe shook his head. "I was. I could get myself into big trouble at her house. I had to leave."

"Another Covelli ready to bite the dust."

"But it can't happen. I don't have anything to offer right now. My life is full of obligations. I need to get this mess about Dad straightened out."

"Why are you making excuses?" Rick asked. "If you care about her…"

"Hell, I've barely been able to keep the business going. If you hadn't been there to bail me out, I don't know what would have happened." He stood up. "Yes, I do. Covelli and Sons would be nonexistent. Everything Dad worked so hard for would have been gone. Because of me."

"No, Rafe. It was because of circumstances. Besides, that's all turned around. The business is getting back on its feet. And remember, the hotel-renovation bid is going to be coming in in another month or two."

"But that's not a sure thing. I can't go after Shelby without knowing there's a future. Until I know I haven't let Dad down." The brothers exchanged a comradely glance. "Until the Covelli name is cleared."

Chapter Six

He was two hours late.

Rafe pulled his truck into the Stewart Manor driveway the next morning and parked behind Rick's Dodge. He grabbed his hard hat and climbed out.

From the second story, Rick walked over to the edge of the porch roof. "Glad to see you could make it to the party."

"Had some things to do," Rafe lied, recalling his restless night, unable to get Shelby off his mind. He hadn't fallen asleep until nearly dawn and didn't hear the alarm when it went off.

"Hope you straightened everything out," Rick said.

"Got it under control," Rafe replied. "How are things coming along?"

"Pretty good. Charlie went to get the replacement windows for downstairs." Rick glanced over his shoulder. "And I'll have this section of the roof finished by noon. Then I'm gonna take the rest of the day off." He grinned. "Since my evening with my wife was...interrupted last night."

"Sorry." Rafe was grateful he had his brother to help him. His thoughts went to Shelby, still trying to figure out how he was going to work around her and not want her. "Thanks for being there."

"Anytime."

"I'd better get to work." He started to his truck to get the new spindles for the porch railing. All of a sudden there was a loud crash from inside the house.

"What the hell?" He swung around and took the steps two at a time and opened the door. "Shelby!" he called, his heart racing.

"I'm upstairs," a faint voice answered.

Rafe raced up the stairs. "Where?"

"In the bedroom."

He hurried through the hall and darted into every room. No Shelby. Then he came to the front bedroom and jerked open the door to find her covered head to toe in plaster dust. The water-damaged ceiling had collapsed and plaster was scattered all over the floor.

He stepped over the pile of debris and went to her. Taking her by the arms, he looked her over. "Are you okay?"

"I'm fine," she said, though she sounded a bit shaken. She began brushing the white powder from her short hair. "I didn't expect the ceiling to give way in such a big chunk."

"You mean this didn't just happen? You were trying to—?"

"You said you couldn't replace it until the old was torn away." She glared at him.

Relieved she was okay, he allowed his anger to surface. "Do you realize how dangerous this is if you don't know what you're doing?"

"I'm not stupid." She jammed her hands on her hips. "And I didn't get hurt."

"You came that close." He held up his finger and thumb

an inch apart for measurement. "You're not even wearing protective clothing." He eyed her jeans and red T-shirt.

Just then Rick rushed into the room and whistled as he glanced around. "Hey, you're making progress, Shelby."

Rafe glowered. "She's creating chaos and endangering herself."

"I am not," she said. "I'm just working on my house. I have every right, don't I, Rick?"

Rick held up his hands. "I'm staying out of this. You two work it out." He backed out the door, closing it behind him.

Rafe turned back to Shelby. "You could have hurt yourself."

"I was careful. I saw it give way and got out of the way."

"This house is over a hundred years old. This is real lath and plaster. Heavy stuff."

Shelby looked away. She didn't want to see the caring she thought she saw in his eyes. He was only angry because she didn't wait for him. Well, he had walked out on her last night without a backward glance. She wasn't going to give him another chance to hurt her again. "I need to get this done," she snapped.

His jaw clenched. "Fine. You want it done, we'll get it done." He went to the window and leaned out to see Josh and Ely working. "Hey, Josh, can you come here a minute?"

The teenager jogged over and glanced up. "What do you need, Mr. Covelli?"

"Do you think you can round up about three of your friends to work the day?"

"Probably. What do you need them for?"

"They're going to haul plaster out from the second floor. Don't bring me any wimps. I need big strong guys who can lift and tote. I'll pay eight dollars an hour and throw in lunch.'' He checked his watch. It was already nine o'clock. "Tell 'em to be here in an hour and ready to work.''

Josh nodded and took off.

"Wait, Rafe. How can I afford to pay them?''

He walked over to the mess and looked up. "You're not. I'm paying them. And I'm going to do this room.''

Shelby had just about had it. "Wait a minute. I'm not going to let you—''

"Don't worry, Ms. Harris, there is no charity involved. But at the rate you're going, I'm better off working for you, than sitting around waiting for you to hurt yourself. So we'll work out a trade. I'll replace the bedroom ceiling and you'll teach me to use a computer.''

Great, Shelby thought. After last night's disaster, she had decided to stay out of Rafe's way. Now she was going to have to spend more time with him. How could she sit next to him and not remember his touch? She looked at him and saw his challenging look. Her only concern was to get this house ready. "Fine. It's a deal.''

He took off his hard hat and placed it on her head. "Wear this hard hat at all times, and don't come into this room without a protective mask over your mouth.''

She nodded. That wasn't unreasonable.

"Another thing. I don't want it advertised that I'm trying to master the computer.''

"Why? Because your ego won't allow you to let a woman teach you anything?''

She expected to see his anger; instead, he tossed her that sexy Covelli grin. "Women have taught me plenty of things, green eyes.'' He reached out and touched her cheek, sending a jolt of heat through her body. "And believe me, I'm a willing student.'' His gazed darkened and she could read his desire. Finally he stepped back. "It's just the less my family knows the better.''

She nodded in agreement and he walked out.

Shelby's knees finally gave out and she sank to the floor. How was she to survive with him around? Her thoughts flashed back to last night and the kiss that had her dreaming about things she shouldn't dream about. She couldn't deny that she had feelings for Rafe, but she wasn't going to act on them. They came from two different worlds. He'd always known where he belonged.

She was desperately trying to make a place for herself. On her own.

The rest of the morning, Shelby left the guys alone as they hauled the plaster out of the bedroom. Rafe had some kind of accordion looking apparatus rigged up that hung from the second story bedroom window down into a dumpster at the side of the house. She could hear the debris fall through the funnel to the bin below. The boys he'd hired were earning their money.

Deciding she was only in the way, Shelby got cleaned up and went downtown to Clark Paint and Wallcoverings. For the next hour, she looked through a selection of wallpaper books. The master bedroom was where she would start her decorating.

Later, Shelby walked by Maria's Ristorante and Angelina spotted her and talked her into coming inside for lunch. After her meal, Shelby showed her wallpaper samples to Maria and Vittoria.

"Oh, this rose print is pretty," Vittoria said. "Hannah Stewart was very fond of roses as you can tell by her garden. Every year she competed in the flower show at the fair."

Maria spoke up. "I couldn't come close to beating her 'Granddaughter's Delight' tea rose. Oh, it was beautiful. A rich pink color."

Shelby hadn't ever heard Ely mention that particular

rose. Maybe it was one of the bushes he couldn't save. "Ely is handling the garden."

Angelina spoke up. "I'd say you had enough to handle trying to keep Rafe in line."

Shelby couldn't help the blush that spread across her cheeks. "We made a deal this morning. I stay out of his way, and he stays out of mine."

"Good idea," Angelina said.

"Oh, stop being so hard on your brother," Maria said. "Rafaele is a good man. He just has a lot of responsibilities." Mrs. Covelli got up to help a customer at the cash register. A tall man in his fifties dressed in a police uniform came in. He had a kind smile, and it was directed at Maria.

Shelby felt Vittoria's hand cover hers. She looked up into dark eyes that mirrored her grandson. "My grandsons are good boys. If Rafe seems gruff it's because he carries a big burden. His shoulders are maybe large, but his heart is soft and filled with pain."

So things weren't as perfect for the Covellis as they looked, she thought, feeling for the family and their tragedy. Her heart ached for Rafe. Last night she saw the pain in his eyes. But Shelby also knew she couldn't afford to think of Rafe as any more than her contractor.

She didn't need to know that he was vulnerable as she was.

About two that afternoon Shelby returned to the house and found four boys eating lunch on the porch. By the looks of the number of bags from the local hamburger joint, Rafe had spent enough money on food to fuel them for the rest of the day.

"Hi, Shelby," Josh said as he stood. "These are my friends, Tom, Jason and Bert. We're all helping Rafe today."

"Nice to meet you boys." The boys, all big and strong-looking, stood and mumbled their hellos.

"I want to thank you for helping out this morning. I'm anxious to get this house livable again."

"We'll help you some more if you need us," Tom said. "I mean, we're out of school for the summer."

"I'll keep that in mind," Shelby said with a smile, then started into the house.

"Is it true this house is haunted?" Jason asked, and got a quick punch in the arm from Bert. "Ouch. Well, my dad said that old Miss Hannah who owned this place…her ghost lives up in the attic." He shrugged. "It's just a story I heard. Like, I don't really believe it."

"Neither do I, Jason." Shelby walked through the door and was greeted by Lucky. After she put her things away, she went upstairs with the cat on her heels and checked on the progress of the front bedroom. She peeked inside and found Rafe working. He had on some sort of coveralls, but they didn't hide his toned body, or the muscles that flexed with his movement on the ladder as he tore away the rest of the ceiling. Her pulse pounded as she raised her gaze to his face. He was wearing a protective mask and a hard hat. He worked skillfully at the task. She recognized a perfectionist when she saw one.

Her smile disappeared as she walked down the hall. How was she going to keep her distance from Rafe when she had to fulfill her part of the bargain and instruct him on using a computer? She knew what happened whenever they got close. But she'd worked with men before and knew how to keep things professional. With Rafe, she'd do her best to stay clear of the man and pray that her royalty check came soon.

Shelby stopped by the master suite and laid out her wallpaper and paint samples on the window seat. Her imagination took over and she began to picture the room with a large area rug and furniture. She already had the old four-poster, but decided she'd make a trip to the attic to see what else was there. She'd retrieve the keys and pick up a flashlight just in case.

After opening the attic door and climbing the narrow staircase, she turned on the lights. There were only two bulbs hung from the ceiling. Maybe she could talk to Rafe about putting in more. She thought about what Jason had said about a ghost living up here. It made her a little leery. She quickly pushed aside the thought and began removing blankets from the stored furniture. The iron bed frame she'd already planned to use in the front bedroom. A scarred dresser that looked like it needed to be refinished was still in good shape. There was also a deacon's bench that could be used in the entry, along with a pedestal table that might work in the upstairs hallway.

Feeling good about her finds, Shelby wandered around the room. She looked up into the rafters and saw an ugly moose head. That would definitely get thrown out. There were pictures, mostly landscapes. She could find a spot for all of them on her bare walls. Then she came upon the door she had noticed during the storm. She tried to open it and remembered it was locked. Going through her ring of keys, she managed to find one that worked. With her heart slamming against her ribs, she turned the handle and pushed it open.

She located a switch on the wall and flipped it on. The room was small, and unlike the attic room, its walls were finished and had once been painted pink. There was a twin bed with a frilly bedspread. Brushing aside a few cobwebs, Shelby walked to the white-painted dresser, on which sat a row of dusty dolls.

"It's a little girl's room," Shelby whispered as she glanced around. "But whose little girl?" She knew that the Stewarts only had the one child, Hannah, and she had never married. Then why was there a room in the attic in a house with five bedrooms?

Shelby went to a closet and pulled open the door. She shined her flashlight inside to find dozens of girls' dresses. Some pink and some white, though all were dingy with dust. On the floor, several pairs of shoes were lined up in a neat row.

"Miss Hannah, what secrets were you hiding from the rest of the world?" Shelby said as she continued her exploration. At the foot of the bed was a white chest. Locked. The tiny key was on the ring and the lid opened with a loud squeak. A musky smell found its way to her nose as she peered in. Neatly folded on top were items from an infant's layette, knit booties and blankets all for a newborn. A baby book had the name "Susan" across the front. Shelby thumbed through the pages, marked with entries about Susan's first year. Shelby put it back, then sorted through several children's books. On the bottom of the chest, under the baby's christening dress, was another book. Shelby pulled out a leather-bound diary.

She sat down on the floor and opened it.

April 5, 1944
Tonight, I met the most wonderful man, Sergeant Paul Braden of the United States Army.

I went with my friend, Betty, to a USO dance in Indianapolis. I almost didn't go because if my parents knew they would never allow me to leave campus. I'm glad that I did, though, because I met Paul. He was very handsome and when he asked me to dance, I had trouble speaking, so I had to nod. When he took me in his arms I trembled so badly I didn't think I could make it around the dance floor. Then he looked at me with his beautiful green eyes and I knew he was a man who would take care of a woman. He held me close and he wouldn't let any of the other soldiers cut in. When the dance ended, he made me promise I'd come back the next weekend. And I know I shouldn't have, but I said yes.

"Shelby!"

She jumped, then yelled back, "I'm up here, Rafe." She closed the diary and quickly put it back in the chest to look at later. She didn't know why, but for now she wanted to keep Miss Hannah's special room to herself. Shelby locked the door and reached the steps just as Rafe was coming up.

He still had a coating of plaster on him, but it didn't detract from his handsome face.

"What are you doing up here alone?"

She didn't like the demanding tone of his question. "I believe I live here, and I can go anywhere in this house I please. I don't need a keeper."

He nodded. "Sorry. Just a habit. Did you find anything interesting?"

"There's a moose head I'm willing to part with if the price is right."

"No, thanks." He went to the furniture stacked in the middle of the attic floor. "There are a few nice pieces here. You're lucky they left them behind."

"I know. I'll have Josh and his buddies carry it all downstairs when you're finished plastering and sanding."

Rafe turned and looked at her. She made a pretty picture in her white tailored blouse with the collar tipped up and nearly touching her short hair. She wore a pair of slim slacks that showed off those long legs. His gaze returned to her face, to her haunting green eyes that had kept him awake most of the night. He hadn't been able to beat down the hunger for her he'd felt all day, either.

"I have to admit I missed you today," he said. "You disappeared for a long time."

"I thought I'd keep out of your hair for a while."

He'd realized that he liked her in his hair. He liked her, period. "I didn't mean to kick you out of your house."

"If it gets the work done, I'll look at wallpaper samples all day and night."

"You went to Clark's?"

She nodded. "He let me take home some books to look over."

He smiled. "Getting anxious?"

"Just a little."

"Well, I finished clearing away the old ceiling. The plasterboard will be delivered Monday and I'll be ready to put it up that afternoon or maybe the next."

"That's wonderful. Do you think I could start painting the master suite?"

"I had an idea I wanted to run by you." He couldn't take his eyes off her. He liked the way her hair framed her face. Her eyes seemed brighter. "Come with me and I'll show you."

He took her hand and they left the attic. He led her into the front bedroom where he'd removed the old ceiling. He went to the closet and opened the door. "This is a good size and it wouldn't take much to turn it into a bath. Nothing fancy, a shower stall, a toilet and sink, then you could even put in a door from the other bedroom so both rooms could share."

"Where would people put their clothes?"

"You could get a wardrobe or an armoire. There are plenty of secondhand and antique stores in the area. Even an estate sale here and there. Jill's been going around looking for things for her and Rick's place."

He was tickled by the way her face lit up. "I like the idea about the bathroom," she said. "That would give me three bathrooms for my five guest rooms." Her expression sobered. "Maybe in a few months. I can't think about adding a bathroom or buying any furniture right now. I—"

Rafe raised a hand to stop her protest. "I know. But how about if I frame it in when I do the ceiling?" He smiled. "No extra charge."

"You mean it?"

He nodded.

"I'd like that," she said, her voice a little husky.

"Consider it done. Then we'll sand the floors and you'll be able to start painting next weekend."

"And wallpaper?"

"Knock yourself out, Ms. Shelby," he said. "The outside of the house should be finished by the middle of next week. Rick will have completed the work on the gables and then he can help me replace the porch spindles and flooring. All you have to do is pick a color for the porch and trim."

"I was thinking about going with cream and forest green."

"Good choice."

"I want to keep Stewart Manor close to how it's always been."

He liked the way she thought. "The town will be happy about that. They were pretty upset when Miss Hannah's cousin let the place go after her death. And since this house is a historical landmark, you qualify for a low-interest loan."

"I already have a mortgage. That's enough for now."

He looked around the room. "You know, I have to admit that your idea of a bed-and-breakfast isn't as crazy as I first thought." His eyes zeroed in on hers. "I'm glad I'm able to help you."

"So am I, but I can't let you continue to work without pay."

He grinned. "I'm not worried about money."

"When would you like to start your computer training?"

He worked hard to keep smiling. "Whenever."

"How about next week?"

"Sure that's fine. Now, would you run by the storefront with me? I have something to show you. We could grab some food on the way." He held up a hand. "Not at Maria's, either. I think you've been interrogated enough by my family. I thought we could pick up some hamburgers and head downtown."

"Okay, but remember I'm a working girl. I need to spend a few hours on the computer."

"Word of honor, I'll have you back in an hour."

She smiled. "And I suppose you never break your word."

They stopped by the Pixie Diner, picked up a couple of hamburgers and chocolate shakes, and headed to Main Street. Rafe parked the truck in front of the storefront that his brother had finished renovating just a few weeks ago. There was a For Lease sign in the window. Shelby, with a designer's eye, critiqued the simple sign and decided to turn it into something more attractive to advertise the office space.

He took her inside and turned on the light. The work they had done was exquisite. The woodwork had all been stripped and refinished. The smooth walls were painted cream and the carpet was blue.

"It's beautiful."

"Thank you. I just wish we could rent it so we'll get a return on our investment. Cousin Tony says to be patient, that the payoff will come." He still looked worried as he walked her through to the rear of the building and they went up a staircase that led to the second floor.

"There is a private entrance from the outside that leads to three apartments on the second floor. They're all rented, and I just moved into the one on the end, so there isn't much inside besides a bed and a sofa." He pulled out his keys and unlocked the door and pushed it open. He switched on the light and allowed Shelby to walk in.

The downstairs color scheme of cream and blue still prevailed with the addition of a navy sofa against the wall. Whitewashed cabinets hung in a small kitchen. He placed the hamburgers on the small round table and pulled out two chairs, then excused himself, and went into the next room. "I'll be right back."

The door closed and within seconds she heard the sound of the shower. Suddenly Shelby felt a shiver throughout her body, knowing that Rafe was naked in the next room. She pushed away the thought and went to the windows covered by wooden blinds. She peeked out and found downtown Main Street below. A light sprinkling of rain made the street glisten, giving everything a freshly washed look. She smiled. Haven Springs was a great town. It must have been wonderful growing up here, where you knew everyone, and everyone knew you. To have a family that was there for you. To have roots.

"Are the hamburgers cold?"

Shelby jerked around to find Rafe standing in the doorway. He had on clean jeans and was buttoning a collared shirt, but not before she got a glimpse of his chest covered with a mat of black hair. She swallowed hard. Oh, my, Rafe Covelli was a beautiful man.

"I said, are the hamburgers cold?" He smiled as if he knew what she was thinking.

She went to the table. "I think they're okay."

Rafe sat down on one of the chairs at the table. "So how do you like what we did with this place?"

"I think you did great."

"I hope you're right, because we've started renovating the building next door."

Shelby picked up a French fry. "Sounds like we're both relying on the tourist trade."

He nodded in agreement and they finished their dinner in quiet conversation. Afterwards, they gathered up the hamburger wrappers and threw them away. Rafe took her hand and led her downstairs again and explained how the town was in the process of rebuilding.

"New business has been coming into town," he said. "We're hoping we'll have a lot more to offer the tourist trade next summer."

Shelby liked his enthusiasm. "I'm sure you will."

He took her to a storage room and turned on a light. Making their way around several boxes, Rafe led her to the corner where there was a large rolltop desk. It was solid oak and in nearly perfect condition.

"She's a beauty, isn't she?"

Shelby ran her hand over the smooth wood grain. "Where did you get it?"

"It was left behind when we bought the place. It was in bad shape then, but I knew there was a beautiful desk underneath."

"You refinished this?"

He nodded. "I came over a few nights a week and worked on her. She's too big to put upstairs. I was hoping I could talk you into giving it a home. You have plenty of places for it and you'd solve the problem of my storing it."

"Me? I couldn't take this. Why not bring it to your office?"

He shook his head. "It would just get damaged there."

Shelby wanted the desk badly. It would go perfectly in the library. "But you've given me so much already, Rafe. I owe you for..."

"Believe me," he jumped in, "you'll be helping me out.

It's a loan. I don't want to sell it, or pay to store it. Look at it as giving this beautiful desk a home."

Shelby hated taking any more handouts. Since she was old enough to pay her own way, she'd swore she never would. "How about if I rent it from you?"

He grinned. "Anyone ever tell you you're too stubborn for your own good?"

She kept a straight face. "No."

"Well, let me go on record. You are one stubborn lady, Ms. Shelby. But if it's so important for you to pay me something then a dollar a month."

She started to argue, and he raised his hand to stop her.

"That's my last offer. If you don't like it, then I'll have to find another home for my desk."

"Over my dead body. I'll take it."

Later, when Rafe pulled up in front of her house, he shut off the engine and turned to look at her. "Thanks for dinner."

"Thank you for…renting me the desk."

"You know I'm going to have to come by every month and collect payment, and if you're late there'll be penalties."

He watched as she bit her lip to keep from smiling. "What kind of penalties?"

Rafe knew he should get out of the truck and walk her to the door. He needed to get rid of temptation, which meant getting away from Shelby Harris. "Severe penalties."

She turned to him. Big mistake. The moonlight caressed her face. "I guess I'll have to make sure that I'm not late on my payments. Oh, how are you going to get it over here?"

"Don't worry about it," he said as his arm stretched out along the top of the seat. He felt as nervous as a high-school kid. "I'll take care of it. I don't want you to get into any more trouble pulling another stunt like today."

Her eyes widened and she opened her mouth to argue. He couldn't resist the temptation and leaned forward, covering her lips with his, swallowing her protest. When she groaned, he pulled her closer, absorbing her softness against his body. He deepened the kiss, feeling his hunger soar. A hunger he knew only Shelby could satisfy. His tongue pushed into her mouth, tasting her desire as his hand roamed over her back. Slowly he moved to the front and stroked her breasts though her blouse. She whimpered and leaned into his caress.

He hurried to undo the buttons of her blouse, and soon his fingers found her bra. He broke off the kiss and moved his mouth down her neck, feeling her tremble.

"Oh, *cara,* what you do to me." He shifted backward, pulling her with him. "You make me crazy."

"Oh, Rafe," she said breathlessly.

Rafe pulled back and could see the desire in her eyes. He kissed her again, and suddenly a pair of headlights brightened the interior of the truck. He held her head against his chest as he looked to see who it was. The car raced through the circular drive, then quickly made its way back to the road.

"Just some kids," he murmured to her.

Shelby raised her head.

But no matter how badly he wanted her, he knew that this was not the time, nor the place. He slowly sat up and began helping her button her shirt. "I'm sorry, Shelby. I shouldn't have taken advantage of you." He felt her tremble again, then stiffen as she pulled away. "Hold it one second, green eyes. It's not that I don't want you. Believe me, the last thing I wanted to do was halt what was happening. I haven't wanted a woman this badly in so long..." He hesitated and tried to gather some composure. He cupped her face in his hands. "I just don't want you to have any regrets."

She nodded. He took a relaxing breath, got out of the truck and came around to her side as she was climbing out. Then he walked her up the steps in silence. She unlocked the door and turned on the light.

"You want me to check out the house?"

"No, I'm fine." She turned around. "Do you still want to start working on the computer next week?"

He shrugged. "I'm not in any hurry." But he decided he wanted to spend time with Shelby and the lessons were a good excuse.

"I can give you three nights a week. Say from seven to nine?"

"Sounds fine. You want to start Monday night?"

She nodded. "But on one condition. That it's strictly business. It isn't a good idea...that we get involved."

Rafe felt hurt tear at his chest. He hadn't been mistaken about what happened in the truck. She'd wanted his kisses. How could she just turn it off?

"I don't think you should kiss me anymore."

That did it. Rafe moved closer. "Then I guess this one is going to have to last a long time," he said as his mouth closed over hers in a searing kiss.

Chapter Seven

Saturday morning, Shelby lay in bed, staring at the newly painted bedroom ceiling. It was the same thing she'd been doing for the past hour. Angry with herself for losing a night's sleep over a silly kiss. Okay, two kisses. A yearning stirred deep in her stomach and she closed her eyes, remembering the feel of Rafe's hands on her skin, his hard body pressed against hers, his mouth—

No! She tossed back the sheet and sat up. She glanced around the sunny yellow bedroom just off the kitchen. This had been her refuge. The place where no one could intrude. Now Rafe Covelli had. His dark eyes, his sexy grin had invaded the privacy of her bedroom. She stood and began to pace. She'd sworn to herself she wouldn't let this happen. She couldn't let herself be attracted to the man, let herself get dependent on him. Sooner or later he'd leave her. She'd be alone again. Better not to ever love than to feel the hurt of rejection.

Shelby pulled off her nightgown and put on a pair of cutoffs and a blue tank top. Slipping her feet into a pair of sandals, she headed for the kitchen, the black-and-white kitten on her heels. After making herself some coffee and feeding Lucky, she went out to the porch and examined the new flooring. Most of the railing spindles had been replaced and soon they could start to paint the trim. She walked down the steps and around back. The sun was shining through the trees and the sight took her breath away. Even a little run-down, Stewart Manor was a beautiful place. She sat down at the metal table on the patio, pulled her feet up and hugged her knees.

This was her home. Her throat tightened as she recalled how hard it had been for her to get here. How hard she'd worked, from the time she left foster care, through college, to her current work. But sheer determination drove her. And nothing was going to stop her from achieving her dream. A home. A place she belonged. A place where no one could send her away, or push her out of.

"Good morning, Miss Shelby."

Shelby jumped. "Oh, Ely, you startled me."

"Sorry, miss." He walked to the table, his limp slowing his progress. "I thought you saw me." He smiled as he set down his thermos. "You must have been daydreaming."

"I guess I was. Please, have a seat."

"Only for a minute. I have to get started before the heat of the day."

"Ely, I don't want you to work too hard and get heat stroke. And I'm going to have to insist on paying you something."

He shook his head. "It's not always about money, Miss Shelby. It's the right thing to do. Stewart Manor has always been a special place to me, and it's a crying shame they let it get so run-down." He pulled off his battered straw hat. "Miss Hannah would be ashamed of the condition of her family home. This place meant so much to her. That's why I need to help bring her rose garden back to life." His kind hazel eyes met hers. "What's the reason you returned to Stewart Manor?"

Shelby frowned. "Returned?"

He gave her a knowing smile. "Years ago, when you were just a little girl, you visited for one summer. I didn't get more than a glimpse of you, but I never forgot those big green eyes."

Shelby was shocked. "You knew I was here?"

He nodded.

"But we only stayed for a few weeks."

The old man's smile disappeared. "You should have stayed longer. Miss Hannah missed you after you left," he said as he stared off toward the garden. "She was never the same." Ely reached for his hat. "Well, I better get to work before the sun gets too hot. Later the gardeners will be coming by to do the tree trimming and mowing."

"Good, let me know how much I owe them," she said. "Oh, and Ely. Do you remember one of Miss Hannah's roses called Granddaughter's Delight?"

He grinned. "Of course. That was her prize-winning tea rose. It was white with deep pink tips—Miss Hannah's favorite colors. But then, all the roses in her garden were either pink or white. It was a beautiful sight. Hopefully we'll be able to get them to bloom once before the season's over."

Even though she'd been only six, Shelby remembered the roses. "I'd like that, Ely."

"I'll see what I can do, miss."

Shelby watched as the old man limped toward the rose arbor. Then her gaze moved to the small cottage she'd stayed in that summer. What was her mother's connection with Hannah Stewart? Had she worked for her? Or was there more? What was the argument that caused her mother to pack up and leave?

Shelby glanced up at the third floor of the main house.

And what was with the little girl's room in the attic? This place held so many secrets. She remembered the diary. Maybe that was where the answers were.

Shelby got up and carried her cup into the house. Grabbing the keys off the hook in the kitchen, she went to the attic and unlocked the door to the secret room. She opened the chest, took out the leather-bound diary and carried it downstairs to her bedroom. She sat on the bed and Lucky jumped up to join her. Leaning back against the pillow, she opened the book and began to read the second entry.

April 12, 1944
Friday finally arrived and I went to the dance. Paul was there, looking so handsome in his uniform. We ended up leaving and going to a movie. We sat in the balcony—where my mother made me swear I'd never go with a young man—and we just held hands at first, then Paul kissed me. My heart raced so hard I thought it would come right out of my chest. I wanted to die when his lips left mine.

He made me promise to meet him the next day, I said I would. Later Betty begged me to be careful. She says guys waiting to be shipped out make a lot of promises they can't keep. I know that Paul isn't like that. He cares about me.

April 13, 1944
Mother will be upset that I didn't come home this weekend, but I wanted desperately to be with Paul. I met him in the booth at Hansen's drugstore, not far from the USO club. We sat there for hours, talking, getting to know each other. We ended up playing with the same straw on the table until our fingers became entwined. Paul seems so loving, so kind. Not like the immature boys from the socially acceptable families

my parents think I should go out with. Once the war ends, he plans to return to Pittsburgh and go to college. He wants to be a lawyer. And I have always wanted to marry a lawyer.

April 18, 1944

All my fears have come true. Paul got his orders and is being shipped overseas next week.

This suddenly turned into our last day together. Will I ever see him again?

I started to cry and Paul took me in his arms and said everything was going to be all right. He said he loved me, and no matter what, he would somehow find a way back to me.

Then he asked me to marry him! I broke down again. I've never been so sad and so happy at the same time. I said yes. But there wasn't time, less than twenty-four hours. Without permission from his commanding officer, we couldn't get married. We'll have to wait until he comes home. Instead, we borrowed his buddy's car and drove to a small hotel outside of town called Gable Inn. Paul rented a room and we spent the night in each other's arms. Before morning we had exchanged our own vows, and became man and wife. When he left me at the bus station, I cried, then prayed that God would keep him safe.

"Oh, my, Miss Hannah," Shelby murmured, "what happened to your young man? Was he killed in the war, or did he love you and leave you?" Sympathy for the woman made Shelby's eyes well with tears.

Shelby began to read on when she heard the doorbell. Marking the page, she slipped the diary into the drawer next to the bed, then rushed through the house to the front door. When she looked through the cut-glass window, she saw Jill Covelli standing on the porch, holding the hand of a small child.

Shelby opened the door. "Jill."

"I know it's a little early for visitors, but Rafe was coming by so I thought we could drop this off to say, 'Welcome to the neighborhood.'" She lifted a plant by the hanger.

"Thank you." Shelby took it just as Rafe came up the walk. Her heart raced as he looked up and their eyes met.

"Morning, Shelby," he said with a curt nod. "I need to take measurements in the bedroom before ordering the drywall."

Shelby nodded, noticing how good he looked, clean-shaven, hair combed neatly off his forehead. The pair of faded jeans he wore, along with a deep burgundy polo shirt, which complemented his olive skin perfectly, made him look as if he'd stepped off the pages of a department-store catalog.

"Sure, come in," she said, stepping aside. "Please, everyone come in."

Rafe brushed past her, barely acknowledging her, then headed up the stairs. She watched until he disappeared. When she looked down again, it was to find Jill eying her closely.

"You have to admit the Covelli men are nice to look at," Jill said.

"I wasn't looking," she began, then glanced away. "It's good to see you. But you didn't need to bring me a gift."

Jill smiled. "Just a little something from Rick and me to add a little color."

"From me, too," the blond boy said.

Shelby leaned down. "Why, thank you. My name is Shelby. What's yours?"

"Lucas," he said proudly.

"Nice to meet you, Lucas."

She stood up again.

"He's precious."

"He has his moments," Jill assured her. "Sorry we didn't come by sooner, but Rick said things have been a mess. And I thought it best to leave you alone for a while." She looked around the entry. "This place is beautiful. And so big."

"You want to have a look around?"

"I'd like that, if it's not too much trouble."

Lucky wandered into the room to see what was going on, and Lucas toddled off after him.

"I hope the cat has a good hiding place."

Shelby shrugged. "Don't worry, Lucky's a survivor."

For the next fifteen minutes she led Jill, who was carrying Lucas, from room to room. But Shelby was anxious to get upstairs to see Rafe. They were in the master bedroom discussing wallpaper samples when Rafe came in.

"If you're going to be a while, I can take Lucas downstairs with me while I call in this order." He picked up his nephew and set him on his shoulders, making it look like the most natural thing in the world. The child giggled and the two walked out of the room, leaving the echo of their happy voices.

"Lucas loves his uncle Rafe," Jill said as she moved to the window seat and sat. "In fact, I always thought Rafe would make a great father. But he's been so busy he doesn't even take time to meet anyone. I mean, there are plenty of women who'd love to go out with Rafe, but not many have interested him. Then you came to town—" Jill raised an eyebrow "—and he's always over here."

"There's been a lot to do." Shelby colored. "But if you're thinking about matchmaking—" she shook her head adamantly "—we're both too independent and stubborn to make a good couple."

"I used to feel that way about Rick. All the Covelli men are strong-willed, a little arrogant and, of course, sexy as sin. But they have hearts of gold. I saw the way you looked at Rafe when he walked up the steps. Your tongue was practically hanging out of your mouth.''

Shelby started to deny it, then changed her mind. ''Like you said, they're easy on the eye.''

''I've also seen Rafe look at you with the same hunger. You'd be perfect for each other.''

''Look, Jill, I'm not looking for a relationship. I've just taken on this big house and I'm trying to get it open for business in a few months. Besides, Rafe and I argue all the time. He doesn't think I can do anything without his help.''

Jill sobered. ''Rafe carries a lot of responsibility. Since his father's death, he feels he has to take care of his mother, grandmother and sister. A strong sense of family.'' She smiled. ''The second-best guy I know. And that's the last thing I'm going to say, 'cause I'm getting far too personal. You barely know me. It's just that this is a small town, and everybody kind of looks after everybody else. A couple of years ago Bob Ashmore, a local policeman, found me outside town. My car had broken down, I had about twenty dollars to my name, and I was three months pregnant.''

Shelby had trouble not reacting. ''I thought Rick...''

''Rick was Lucas's father? Well, he is in all the ways that count. But the fact is, Lucas's father left me. He didn't want to be bothered with a kid. My parents weren't ready to take me back home, either. It was the Covelli family who opened their arms and their hearts. They're free with their friendship and they'll never desert you.''

Shelby wanted to believe Jill, but experience told her a different story. People always disappointed you. Better to keep your guard up.

''I hope you feel at home in Haven Springs. If there's anything you need, don't hesitate to call. Maria said the same.''

Jill rose from the window seat when Rafe returned with

her sons. "C'mon, Lucas, Daddy's going to take us to the lake to swim."

"Swim!" The boy's face lit up.

"Thanks for stopping by," Shelby said. "And for bringing the lovely plant." She looked at Rafe. "Did you get everything measured?"

He nodded, his eyes not making a connection with hers. "They'll deliver everything Monday morning."

"Thanks for doing this for me."

He shrugged. "No problem."

Shelby walked everyone to the door.

"Oh, by the way," Jill said, "I forgot to ask you. Rick and I are having a barbecue out at the lake tomorrow and you're invited."

Shelby began to fidget. "But...but I can't. I don't know my way around and it would be better if—"

"I won't take no for an answer. Rafe will drive you out so you won't get lost."

Shelby's gaze darted to Rafe. He didn't look happy at the prospect. But she couldn't turn down the invitation. "What time?"

"Around two, and bring your swimsuit."

Jill walked off and Rafe stood there for a minute, thinking how he'd like to strangle his new sister-in-law. He looked at Shelby. "Be ready to go by one."

Shelby nodded.

Rafe marched to the truck. With each step, he was getting more annoyed with Jill. He knew she meant well, but he didn't need the interference. He climbed in as Jill finished fastening Lucas in his seat.

"What you're doing isn't going to work."

"I have no idea what you're talking about."

"You planned this barbecue just to play matchmaker." He gave her a sideways glance. "It's not going to work."

"Never say never, Rafe. Shelby Harris is a nice woman, not to mention, beautiful."

Rafe sighed. "Well, that doesn't mean I'm going to do anything about it."

Jill looked toward the house. "She could use a friend, then. She has so much sadness in her eyes it makes me want to cry."

Rafe had noticed that, too. "Why should she be lonely? She has family. She could have moved closer to them, instead of coming here and turning my life upside down."

"I had family, too, when I came here, but you know everything wasn't perfect between us. You know that my dad didn't even come to see Lucas until last spring." She shook her head. "No, I'd bet that Shelby Harris is all by herself. And I remember what that feels like. But I was lucky, because I had friends to fill the empty spaces in my life."

Rafe reached over and took his sister-in-law's hand. "You just kind of grew on us."

"Well, then let Shelby grow on you, too. Find out why she's always pushing you away."

That was the problem. Shelby Harris had already grown on him. Far more than was safe.

The following morning Shelby awoke to another sunny day. Praying for rain hadn't helped a bit; it was perfect for a barbecue. She dressed in a pair of cutoffs and a red blouse, telling herself these clothes were good enough. Today she planned to make it known to everyone that there was nothing going on between her and Rafe.

She didn't have to worry about Rafe. Yesterday he'd practically ignored her, making his feelings quite clear. And of course, she wasn't interested in him, either, other than as her contractor.

At one o'clock Rafe pulled into the drive and Shelby

went out to meet him. He was dressed in khaki shorts, a faded blue T-shirt and beat-up tennis shoes. He politely helped carry her contributions to the feast—a cooler of soda and her special cheesy potatoes.

When they set off for the lake, Rafe was silent. Shelby knew he'd only brought her along because Jill had forced him into it. Well, she was used to being pushed off on people who didn't want her. She could deal with Rafe's silence for a few hours.

After a short while Rafe sighed and said, "You know, my family isn't going to put up with us not getting along."

What was he talking about? "We get along."

He glanced at her. "You know what I mean. They want us to *really* get along."

She looked away. "I'm not very good at this, Rafe. I haven't dated much...so I don't play the game."

His eyes narrowed. "You're kidding about the dating, right?"

She shook her head. "No."

"The guys in Louisville must be blind."

His words thrilled her. "I don't know if they were or weren't. I was too busy working and going to school to pay any attention."

"Didn't your family help out?"

She hated these questions. "They couldn't afford to. So I applied for student loans."

"I took out a few of those myself. Then I worked my butt off for Dad during the summer." He finally smiled and her stomach did a somersault.

"What's your degree in?" she asked.

"History."

She was surprised but tried not to show it. Apparently she didn't succeed.

"You're shocked that a guy like me would be interested in history?"

"No, it's only that you…"

"Work as a carpenter?"

"Yes."

He turned off the highway onto a side road. A few yards up he pulled onto the shoulder and shut off the engine. Then he faced her. "My dad had this idea that his kids should get a degree, no matter what it was in. I love being a carpenter—that's all I ever wanted to be since I was a kid." His jaw tensed. "I've always wanted to work alongside my old man. And I did, for a few years, anyway. Until he was killed."

Shelby saw the pain etched across his handsome face, and she touched his hand, trying to comfort him. "He'd be proud of the work you're doing."

"Think so?"

She nodded.

He turned his palm up and captured her fingers, sending a warm rush through her. "You know, I thought by now the pain would go away, but it hasn't. Maybe it's because the accident was caused by someone's greed and foolishness." He tipped his head back against the seat.

His pain reawakened Shelby's. No matter how long it had been, she still missed her mother. The loneliness was there every day.

"My family means a lot to me, Shelby." His gaze met hers again. "I know they can be overbearing and pushy, but they mean well, and I love them. I'm apologizing now, because when we arrive at the cottage, they're going to be all over us, trying to make us a…couple."

She hated that the idea made her pulse race.

He leaned closer. "If we convince them we already like each other, then they won't be trying so hard to get us together. I know you asked me not to kiss you, but I may have to break that promise."

Shelby swallowed. Her mouth was tingling now, just at

the thought of his lips on hers. She drew a needed breath. "Do you mean you're going to kiss me?"

He shrugged. "There may not be any other way. Would that be so horrible?"

"No," she squeaked, then cleared her throat. "But isn't that being dishonest to your family? Letting them think something that isn't true?"

"It's not an out-and-out lie. Besides, I'll be going to your place when you teach me to work on the computer. They'll think there's more going on." He leaned even closer, so close his breath caressed her face. "So if we work hard at convincing them today, maybe they'll stop trying to throw us together."

"How?"

"Maybe like this." His mouth touched hers, then he pulled back. She gasped as a tingling feeling shot through her.

"Easy, Shelby. I only want a quick rehearsal. Just so when I kiss you in front of everyone, you won't react like you're afraid of me."

"But I'm not afraid," she whispered.

"Maybe you should be."

Rafe captured her head between his hands, then closed his mouth over hers, lightly at first, not wanting to scare her, but fighting with himself not to devour her. She tasted so sweet, so fresh, he couldn't resist, and he thrust his tongue into her mouth. She whimpered and his arms slid around her back and drew her against him. Shelby's hands moved up his chest and circled his neck, and she pressed her body against his; he could feel her pebble-hard nipples against his chest. Fighting the urge to rip off her clothes, he tightened his hold.

Suddenly a horn sounded and they jumped apart as a black car pulled up beside them. Damn. It was Tony and Angelina. They waved, then continued on their way.

"Well, looks like we've been discovered. By the time we get to the cottage, my sister will have told the whole family." Shelby could see the desire in his dark eyes. "Come on, it's time to face the music." He restarted the truck.

Rafe drove the next mile to the south shore of the lake. At last the two-story white cottage came into view. The lake was about fifty yards down a slope from the cottage and a pier stretched out over the glassy water. Farther out, a raft with a diving board bounced up and down from the boat waves coming into shore. Rafe parked next to the other family cars. He stepped out of the truck and hurried to open the door for Shelby.

"It's so beautiful here," she said as she slung her tote over her shoulder.

Rafe grabbed the cooler and the covered dish from the back. "Come on," he said, then walked straight to Nonna Vittoria, seated in the rocker on the porch. She greeted him in Italian, letting him know she approved of his guest.

When he reached her side, he leaned down to kiss her. "Hello, Nonna. You remember Shelby."

His grandmother's dark eyes lit up as she gripped Shelby's hand. "Of course. So nice to see you again."

"I'm very glad to be here," Shelby said as she gave Nonna a dazzling smile.

Just then Angelina rushed up onto the porch, Tony not far behind her. "Hi, Shelby." She grinned. "I'm so glad you came."

"I have Jill to thank for the invitation."

Rafe watched as Tony pushed in closer. "Hi, I'm Tony Covelli." He stuck out his hand and Shelby took it. "I'm glad you could make it today." He turned on the charm. "I've heard so much about you I feel I know you already."

Rafe felt his irritation building. He gave the covered dish to his sister, then placed his arm around Shelby's shoulders.

"Back off, cuz. She's taken." He caught the wistful look in Shelby's green eyes and suddenly wished it was true.

Tony glanced between them, then smiled. "Guess I'm too late again." He turned to Shelby. "Let me know when you get tired of this big guy. I'll be around."

Rafe wanted to order his cousin to stay far away from Shelby, but knew he didn't have the right. But at least for today, he did.

Shelby felt herself tremble as Rafe continued to hold her. She took a deep breath, wishing she could run away. She wasn't good at game playing, and she had absolutely no experience when it came to flirting.

Shelby heard her name called. She turned to see a smiling Maria walking with little Lucas along the water's edge. Shelby waved.

Rick and Jill came out dressed in their swimsuits. "We're going for a swim. Come join us," Jill said as her husband grabbed her hand and pulled her along. "Take any of the bedrooms upstairs to change in." She gasped when Rick swung her up in his arms and began running toward the water.

"You brought a suit, didn't you?" Rafe asked Shelby.

"Yes, but I don't know if I'll go in the water."

"Come on, Shelby," Rafe whispered. "Let yourself go. Or are you afraid you can't keep up?"

One of the few things Shelby hadn't been deprived of as a product of the foster-care system was swimming. She had spent the summers going to public pools. "I think I can keep up. Give me a minute to change, and I'll give you a run for your money."

Rafe tossed her the sexy grin that made her weak in the knees. "Should we make a bet on who comes out on top?"

Chapter Eight

Wearing her red blouse as a cover-up, Shelby walked out of the bedroom upstairs where she'd changed and down the stairs. She stopped in the large kitchen and asked Nonna Vittoria if she needed any help with the meal. The family matriarch hugged her.

"You go out and have fun with my grandson. He is a good boy." The older woman smiled and sent Shelby on her way.

Feeling as if all eyes were on her, Shelby made her way to the water's edge where Angelina was sunbathing in a two-piece suit.

"You know this isn't fair," Angelina said. "Your legs come up to my waist."

"Believe me, I'd gladly give you a few inches of my height. I was always the tallest kid in my class in high school."

"And I was always the shortest," Angelina said, laughing.

Shelby noted the brunette's luscious curves and had trouble feeling sympathy for her. "I don't think you have much trouble drawing attention from men."

"You're forgetting Rick and Rafe, then throw in cousin Tony. They won't let a man near me."

Shelby had to smile. It would be nice to have someone be protective of her. "You going in the water?"

Angelina shook her head. "Think I'll work on a tan. But if you find an unattached guy who isn't a Covelli, send him to shore."

"Will do." Shelby glanced around. No one was paying any attention to her. Rafe was out at the diving platform, too busy horsing around with Rick and Tony to notice her. That suited her fine, for she needed some time to herself, and a relaxing swim would work out some of the tension from long hours at the computer. She pulled off her blouse, exposing her one-piece black suit. After laying the shirt on the pile of towels, she ran into the lake. The water felt cool and refreshing as she dove under. When she surfaced, she began her long, lazy strokes.

Suddenly she felt someone grab her around the waist and pull her under. She came up fighting.

"Hey, it's me," Rafe said as he cradled her against him. "I didn't mean to frighten you."

He turned her around, his hand on her waist, their legs brushing intimately. "I wasn't frightened," she said. "Just surprised."

He grinned. "Then I'll let you see this coming." He lowered his head and his mouth came down on hers in a kiss. By the time he released her, she was gasping for air, but managed to regain her footing on the sandy lake bottom.

"Rafe. What are you doing?" She moved back from him in the shoulder-deep water.

There was a mischievous glint in his dark brown eyes. "If you have to ask, then I wasn't doing it right. Besides, we're supposed to be putting on a show for the family. Come with me," he said as he took her hand and they made their way to the swimming buoy that kept the boats out of the swimming area.

They grabbed hold of the rope. "Now isn't this better," Rafe said as he leaned his head down to nuzzle her neck.

Shelby put her hand against his bare chest to stop him and glanced around. Not a soul was paying any attention to them. "Rafe, you can stop. There's no one watching."

He leaned closer as his hands moved up and rested just under her breasts. "I am, *cara*. I've been staring at you since you walked out the door in your swimsuit. You have the most beautiful legs I ever laid eyes on." His lips made contact with her neck. "You cause a man to conjure up a fantasy or two. And I'm not going to let you out of my sight." His mouth went to her shoulder and Shelby shivered. "My cousin Tony looked entirely too interested in you."

She opened her mouth to tell him to stop but couldn't find the words.

His head rose to hers. "Your eyes are the most incredible green." His gaze lowered. "And your mouth—" his finger traced along her top lip, then the bottom "—is perfection." He captured her lips in a searing kiss that didn't end until she was clinging to him shamelessly.

Rafe's hands moved over her, caressing her breasts through her thin suit, then pulling her legs around his waist. She gasped from the friction of his body as he moved against hers.

"Oh, Rafe," she whimpered.

"You feel so good, *cara*," he murmured against her mouth. "I can't get enough of you."

She wanted to give him more, more than she'd ever given to any man. She closed her eyes, feeling her heart pounding in her chest, then reality struck as she heard the sound of a voice coming closer. Rafe pulled back, but held her protectively as Rick swam toward them.

"Hey, you two," he said. "We've been yelling at you."

Shelby felt the heat rise to her cheeks. Could the family see them from the shore?

"I guess you didn't hear." Rick tossed a wicked grin at his brother. "Come on in. We're about to eat. And you know how Nonna is about being there for the blessing."

"In a minute," Rafe said.

Rick nodded and swam off.

Shelby covered her face. "I'm so embarrassed."

"Why? A few months ago Rick and Jill were doing the same thing. Rick doesn't think there's anything wrong with us kissing." He placed another on her lips. "I'm sorry, Shelby, I can't keep my promise to you."

Shelby felt her breathing stop. "What promise?"

"I can't stop kissing you, nor do I want to. So you better tell me now to take a hike, because that's the only way I'm going to stop."

She knew it was a mistake, but she couldn't push him away. She loved being in his arms, couldn't resist his kisses. "I don't want you to…stop. But…"

He smiled. "I promise I'll go slow, but I think we need to see where this leads."

Shelby stiffened. She knew she couldn't let this lead anywhere. Rafe would just find out that she'd been lying all along, and that she couldn't fit into his life. "Maybe we shouldn't plan on anything too…permanent."

He placed his finger over her mouth. "One day at a time."

She wanted to believe it was possible, but she knew better.

Suddenly there was commotion on the shore, and they looked that way to see his family waving at them. "We'll finish this later." He released her and they swam back toward the shore.

Rafe was determined not to let Shelby push him away again. Tonight they would talk, and he'd convince her that they were meant to be together.

When they reached the beach he handed Shelby a towel, then took her hand and they walked to the porch. In addition to his family, he saw Billy Jacobs, the PI Rick had hired.

Dressed in jeans and a Western shirt, Billy held his cowboy hat in his hand. "Sorry to bother you on the weekend, Rafe." They shook hands.

"Not a problem."

"I thought you and your family would want to know that we finally nailed Peter Hardin."

The women gasped. Rafe glanced at Rick's surprised look, then they both turned back to Billy. "For real?"

The private investigator from Texas grinned and nodded. "He was arrested last night for possession of cocaine. But not before Hardin confessed to an undercover cop that he'd been taking money for top-grade lumber, but shipping out substandard and using the cash to buy drugs. Pete, Jr. also admitted that he stopped after your father's accident."

Rick cursed and Jill went into his arms.

Billy looked at Maria. "There's no doubt that Peter Hardin was responsible for Rafaele Covelli's death."

Rafe hugged his mother. Nonna blessed herself and murmured a prayer in Italian. Tony held Angelina as her tears began to fall. Rafe felt his own build behind his eyes, but he didn't want to fall apart. Not now. Not when he'd made it this far. It wasn't over yet.

"When's the trial?" Rafe asked.

"He's being arraigned tomorrow."

Rafe clenched his fists. He looked at his brother, knowing there was only one way for them to have closure. Rick nodded in agreement. "Rick and I want to be there."

Both Rafe and Shelby were silent on the drive back to town. It was almost a relief to Shelby when Rafe pulled the truck into the driveway. He carried her things through the back door into the kitchen, where he set her empty dish on the counter.

"I want to thank you for a wonderful day," she said.

"Thanks for coming," he said. His eyes bleak. "Sorry we had to cut it short."

She went to him. "I understand, Rafe." She wanted to comfort him, but she didn't know how. All her life she'd stood back and watched so she wouldn't have to give emotionally. Now when Rafe needed her, she was lost.

"Well, I'd better go," he said, and turned toward the door.

She didn't want him to leave. She rushed across the room. "Will you stop by tomorrow night so we can begin work on the computer?"

"I'm not sure," he said. "Can I let you know?"

Her heart sank. "Of course." She stepped closer. He was so tall she had to look up and his broad shoulders nearly filled the doorway. And she knew he held the weight of the world on those shoulders. But who held Rafe when his world fell apart? Shelby knew only too well what it was like to be alone.

"Good night, Shelby," he said, and started to turn away.

Without thinking, Shelby reached for his hand and stopped him. When he looked at her with questioning eyes, she said, "You don't have to go…"

Rafe swallowed hard. "What are you saying, Shelby?"

She boldly moved into the circle of his arms. "You don't need to be alone tonight, Rafe." She reached up and kissed his jaw. "Let me help you…"

Rafe's eyes glowed with an inner fire, then his mouth lowered, smothering hers in a hard, hungry kiss. Shelby's knees nearly buckled, but he pulled her tightly against him. Feeling the aching throbbing low in her stomach, Shelby gave back eagerly, wanting and needing Rafe as much as he wanted and needed her.

Finally he broke off and pulled back. "Your mouth," he groaned. "I hurt you."

"No, you could never hurt me." She gazed into his eyes and saw a sadness that nearly broke her heart.

"It's okay, Rafe. I know you're in pain." She brushed her fingers along his cheek. "I just want to be here for you."

"Oh, Shelby," he murmured, and pulled her against him again. Locking his arms around her, he began to sob. Shelby held him as he cried for the father who had loved his family and died so tragically. Shelby cried for never knowing her own father and never getting the chance to feel that kind of love.

She didn't know how much time had passed when Rafe raised his head. Tears still streaked his eyes. She brushed them away. He lowered his head and kissed her wet cheek, tasting her tears, then found her mouth again.

Finally he pulled back and looked at her. He couldn't remember wanting a woman like this before. "I want you, *cara*. I think I've wanted you from the moment I first saw you."

Rafe felt her tremble and knew she was afraid. Hell, so was he. Then surprisingly, she took his hand and walked him through the doorway that led to her bedroom. Releasing him, she turned on the lamp next to a double bed, creating a soft glow. He pulled her into his arms. When his mouth came down on hers again, she eagerly returned the fervent kiss.

He drew back and watched as her breasts moved up and

down with her rapid breathing. Then, her eyes all soft and inviting, she sat down on the edge of the bed. Rafe knew that every promise he'd made to her and himself had just been broken. He was involved. Deeply. Shelby held out her hand and he quickly eliminated the space between them. His mouth covered hers, this time the kiss was hotter and sweeter than ever before, and they ended up lying side by side on the mattress.

With shaky hands, Rafe undid her blouse and bra. With a groan, he dipped his head and closed his mouth over one bare breast and sucked gently until her nipple hardened. Shelby arched against him, her fingers in his hair, tugging him closer. He removed his shirt and pulled her against his naked chest.

"Tell me if you want me to stop, Shelby," he murmured as he felt her tremble in his arms. His hands moved to her shorts and he tugged at the zipper, then slipped a hand inside. Suddenly she stiffened.

"What's wrong, *cara*?" he whispered.

She shook her head, then glanced away.

He refused to let her hide, and with his fingers on her chin, he made her look at him. "Please, tell me, did I do something wrong?"

Her green eyes widened. "You didn't do anything wrong," she assured him. "It's just…I've never been with a man."

Rafe tried not to show his shock, but it was hard to hide. He was thrilled and terrified at the same time. "You've never made love?"

Her eyes brimmed with passion. "No," she whispered.

He groaned inwardly, using every ounce of restraint he could muster to stop. He moved his hand to her face and cupped her cheek. "How did that happen?"

"Easy. Nobody wanted me," she said as she tried to pull away.

He refused to release her. "Whoa, don't get skittish on me. I only meant that you're a very desirable woman. And I'm damn honored you chose me, but…" He swallowed back the sudden dryness in his throat. She was going to give herself to him.

"But no thanks, right?" she choked out.

"God, Shelby, if only you knew how hard…" He stopped and managed to smile. "I mean, difficult it is not to jump your beautiful body, but I'm not going to take advantage of you like this. I care too much about you."

She sat up and began buttoning her blouse. "I guess you'll want to leave, then."

Rafe wished he'd kept his mouth shut. He touched her back and she tensed once again. "I'm not going anywhere unless you want me to. I don't want to be alone tonight. I liked it when you held me earlier. I'd like to return the favor. I want to hold you, Shelby. Sometimes the nights can be so lonely, and it's just nice when someone is there. I want you to be that someone."

"You really want to stay?"

He nodded. "Come here." He tugged her down beside him again and laid her head on his shoulder. "Just close your eyes and I'll be here for you. We'll be here for each other."

The next morning Shelby rolled over and reached out. Rafe was gone. She could still smell his scent on the pillow—and that of a rose from her garden along with a note.

"I hated to leave you, but didn't want the neighbors to gossip. I'm going to Louisville. I'll see you later. Thank you for a special night. Rafe."

Shelby smiled. For the first time in a long time, she was letting herself open up to someone. She knew better, knew she could get hurt, but when it came to Rafe Covelli, her common sense left her. Her heart ruled her thinking.

Smiling, she climbed out of bed and headed for the shower. Rafe was coming over tonight, so she wanted to get her work done before then. She turned on the shower and had a quick shampoo and wash, then got out. Putting on clean jeans and a shirt, she headed to the front of the house and her computer. That's when she saw a man coming up her front porch. She opened the door.

"I'm looking for Ms. Shelby Harris," he said.

"I'm Shelby Harris."

About sixty, the man was dressed in a dark business suit. "I'm very happy to make your acquaintance, Ms. Harris. I'm Bently Wolfe, the president of the Haven Springs Historical Society. We were pleased to hear that Stewart Manor was going to be restored and opened as a bed-and-breakfast."

"I'm glad you approve, Mr. Wolfe. But it's going to be a while before the inside is finished and I'm ready for business."

"That's what I wanted to talk to you about. Since your house once belonged to one of the town's founding fathers it's an historical landmark. We have a fall festival where we turn back the clock and have tours through the Victorian homes in the neighborhood. We have fifteen on the list."

"I would love to open my house, Mr. Wolfe, but I don' have enough furniture to fill the rooms."

He smiled. "Well, we'll have to work on that and see what we can do." He glanced up at the house. "Stewart Manor would sure be a big draw on the tour this year. I've noticed that the grounds are taking shape again. I know that would have pleased Miss Hannah."

"You can thank Ely Cullen for doing such a good job."

Mr. Wolfe handed her a business card. "I'll get back to you on the date of the festival. Think about being a part of it, even if we can only tour the gardens."

"Thank you, Mr. Wolfe. I'll let you know."

As he returned to his car, Charlie, who was finishing the porch flooring, said, "It's a fun time of year in Haven Springs. No cars are allowed on these streets for three days, and we ride around in horse and buggies. I heard that this year they're even going to include the downtown area. Bet Rafe would be willing to help you get ready. And it's a great way to meet more of the townspeople."

Haven Springs was a wonderful town, and Shelby wanted to meet her neighbors. She also knew that Rafe was always willing to help her. But she had to stand on her own. Unlike her mother, Shelby couldn't let a man control her life.

That afternoon Rafe sat in his brother's Dodge Durango on the way back from Louisville, still trying to absorb what had happened. They hadn't said much about what had taken place in the courtroom.

Rafe looked over at Rick. "I still can't believe that jerk is going to get off with manslaughter."

"I'm just as angry as you are, bro," Rick said, "but there's nothing we can do about it. Just make sure that when the trial comes around, we have a say in his sentencing. Judges are listening to injured families now."

Rafe rubbed his temples. "I just wish I could have done something back then. Maybe Dad wouldn't have died."

Rick waved a hand in the air. "And I wished I had stayed home all those years and been a better son." Rick took his eyes off the interstate a second and glanced at his brother. "Dammit, Rafe, none of this is doing any of us any good. Dad's gone, and we can't change that. We need to move on. I know Dad would be upset if he knew we'd spent so much time being bitter. So beginning today we have to promise we're going to forgive ourselves for not being perfect sons."

Rafe chuckled. "How in the hell did you get so wise?"

Rick smiled. "Hell, it took a good woman who loves me and believes in me. Sure makes life a helluva lot easier."

Rafe thought back to the night before and what it was like to have Shelby so near. How good it felt to lean on someone. And how close they'd come to making love. A shot of heat rushed through him.

"Hey, bro, don't you think it's time you let yourself get involved in a relationship?"

"Maybe, but I'm not exactly in a position to think—and I stress *think*—about settling down with…someone. The business isn't exactly rolling in bids or money."

"Tony rented the office space downtown."

"When?" Rafe sat up straighter.

"He called before I left this morning. He'd been looking for you, but said you weren't answering your phone."

Rafe hadn't gotten home until six a.m., with just enough time to quickly shower and get dressed before Rick picked him up. How he'd hated leaving Shelby's bed. "Did we get what we were asking?"

Rick nodded. "And they signed a two-year lease."

Rafe was happy, but the rent money still wasn't enough to put his mind at ease. "We need jobs. The facade restorations are about finished, and we haven't heard anything yet on the Haven Springs Hotel bid."

"Just hold on. I have a feeling when this story hits the papers, things will start to turn our way. You know when Pete Hardin apologized for his son, he promised he'd do anything to help Covelli and Sons. So don't you go giving up on Shelby. She's a special woman."

Rafe knew how special Shelby was, but he still couldn't offer her anything. All he had was a business still in the red, with just enough income to make the payroll. Tony said it would take time. But could he ask Shelby to stick around? Suddenly he couldn't wait to get home. He smiled. He had someone waiting for him.

"Does that stupid grin mean you aren't going to be interrupting my nights with your bellyaching anymore?"

"Could be," Rafe said. "But you know we still have to deal with the Covelli curse."

That afternoon Shelby was drawn to Hannah's diary again. She took it out of the drawer and sat down on the bed to read it.

May 25, 1944

Usually I love coming back to Haven Springs for summer break, but not this time. I've only gotten one letter from Paul since he left. I know that his unit shipped out, and he could have gone anywhere—Europe, Africa, even the Pacific. I want to cry every time I think about him in danger. I miss him so. Why couldn't we have met sooner so we could have had more time together? Only a few weeks, but I knew right from the start that I loved Paul, that I would love him until the day I died. Please God. Just bring him back to me.

June 1, 1944

I wake up in the morning and I think about Paul and wonder if he's thinking about me. I mope around the house and my mother keeps asking me what's wrong. How can I tell her I fell in love and am miserable? She wouldn't approve because Paul doesn't come from the right social background. Well, I don't care. I love him.

June 7, 1944

It was all over the news about D day. Thousands of troops landing on Omaha Beach. So many men were killed but all I could think about was Paul. I got sick to my stomach and spent the day in bed praying that

God had kept him safe.

June 20, 1944
I woke up this morning and was sick again, like I've been for the past two weeks. I called Betty and we drove to Indianapolis to the doctor. But I didn't need a doctor to tell me I'm carrying Paul's baby. I want to cry with joy, but it breaks my heart that I can't tell Paul.

June 30, 1944
I'm not showing yet, but I know I have a life growing inside me. I wrote Paul to tell him the wonderful news, but it's hard to know when and if mail reaches him. I've only gotten one letter from him and I've read it over and over again.

July 1, 1944
My world ended today. I received a letter from another soldier in Paul's unit. He wrote that Paul was killed on D day. He spoke my name before he died and said he loved me. I fainted, and my mother called the doctor and discovered I was with child. I explained how much I loved Paul, but she won't hear any of it. She's sending me away to have the baby in secret. Then she told me that I'll have to give my baby up. Paul's baby. I'll die first.

Shelby closed the diary, her heart thudding painfully in her chest. How Hannah had loved her baby! Shelby climbed off the twin bed and looked around the tiny attic room.

"You made this room a shrine to your child. Oh, Hannah, was this the only place you could express your pain at losing your little girl? The one you named Susan Pauline?''

Shelby couldn't help but wonder how it would feel to have someone love her as much as Hannah loved her daughter. How much her little girl was wanted. Why couldn't Nola Harris have loved her daughter as much? Why were the men in Nola's life more important than her own child?

Shelby remembered the day her mother gave her away. She was only six, but that hadn't made any difference to Nola. She said she was sick and couldn't keep her daughter, then just walked away.

Shelby heard a noise downstairs and checked her watch. *Rafe.* She ran out of the room with Lucky on her heels, locked the door and hurried down the steps to the second floor. She heard Rafe call her name.

"I'm up here," she yelled, hurrying along the hall to the staircase. She stopped at the top when she saw Rafe standing at the bottom. He was dressed in a dark brown suit, a white shirt, with a blue-and-brown-striped tie hung loosely around his neck. Her heart began to pound. He was gorgeous.

"Hi," he said. "I was worried you'd get tired of waiting for me."

She shook her head, nervous, remembering what had happened between them last night, wondering what to do next.

Rafe put his foot on the bottom step. "Woman, are you coming down, or am I going to have to come up and get you?"

She smiled, knowing her knees were getting weaker by the second. "Maybe we can meet in the middle."

Before she could move, Rafe had taken the steps two at a time and was standing before her. "It's been fourteen hours since I left your bed. I need to feel you in my arms."

He drew her against him. "Kiss you..." His mouth closed over hers in a hungry kiss. By the time he released her, they were both having trouble standing.

"Did you miss me today?" he asked.

She nodded.

Rafe grinned and couldn't take his eyes off her. She looked beautiful. "Nice to know I'm appreciated." He hugged her. "I thought about you all day."

She pulled back and they started down the steps. "How did things go in Louisville?"

"Peter Hardin goes to trial in two months, but the DA is going after a manslaughter charge. He probably won't do much jail time."

"I'm sorry, Rafe." She took his arm as they walked into the front room. "Tonight I'm going to take your mind off everything."

"Oh, this sounds promising," he said as she led him past the sofa to the desk and computer.

She placed a quick kiss on his lips, and before he could grab her, she moved out of his reach and pulled the cover off the computer. "I'm going to teach you the basics."

He groaned. "Can't we put this off till another time?"

"I think this might be for the best. Last night...last night we went a little too fast."

Rafe frowned at her. Last night with Shelby in his arms had been wonderful. "You regret my staying?"

She shook her head. "We've only known each other a short time. I'm just afraid..."

"That I'm going to pressure you into something you're not ready for?"

She glanced away. "Can't we be friends first?"

His heart sank, the same line he'd gotten years ago from Jeannie. "Okay, I get the message." He started to walk away.

"Rafe, no." She grabbed his arm. "Please don't leave. I only meant—"

"I know a kiss-off when I see one."

She stiffened. "I wouldn't know how to kiss off anyone, you big oaf. As you discovered, I'm not exactly experienced. Not enough for you, anyway. So…so just go." She turned away.

Rafe felt like the world's biggest jerk. Somehow Shelby had made it to nearly thirty without a serious relationship with a man. And last night she had offered herself to him to help erase his pain. Now he was causing hers.

"Shelby, I'm sorry. You're plenty for me. You're all I've been thinking about, all I fantasize about. I—"

She placed a finger against his lips. "I learned a long time ago not to expect much. I have everything I need right now, except maybe you sitting in that chair and your hand on the mouse." She gave him a stubborn look. "I *will* teach you how to run a computer."

Her smile made heat spread through his body. "And I want to teach you…" He whispered his suggestion in her ear and was rewarded with her involuntary shiver.

"You bad boy!" she gasped. "Does your mother know you talk like that?"

He groaned. "You had to bring my mother into this."

She smiled sweetly. "Good, now I have your undivided attention." She pushed him into the desk chair. "For the next few hours I'm going to whip you into shape."

"Now, I like the sound of that."

Chapter Nine

On Tuesday Rafe had arrived early to start work on the front-bedroom ceiling. Besides a sexy grin and a quick kiss when he'd come through the door, he hadn't come downstairs all morning. And Shelby had stayed out of the way, too, spending her time at the computer designing a special surprise for Rafe.

Stretching, she leaned back in her chair, listening to the high-pitched whine of the power saw overhead.

She thought back to last night with Rafe. He had kept his promise to her to cool things between them. He had been genuinely interested in learning and sat patiently next to her as she went over the commands of the computer program.

A shiver of pleasure raced through her when she recalled the few times they'd gotten sidetracked. Rafe's kisses had thrilled her; no man had ever made her feel this way. She'd never let a man get close enough, but she couldn't seem to stop herself when it came to Rafe Covelli.

Her heart began to pound as she rose and began to pace

the room. Couldn't she let this happen? She'd always told herself she would never be like her mother. Never be so weak that she'd let a man control her life. Shelby walked to the mantel and searched the row of family pictures. She stared at the strangers' faces, wishing they were really her family, wishing she had aunts and uncles. What if there had been a grandmother, someone who could have raised her after her mother left? There was no one. Shelby had been and still was alone.

She glanced around the large parlor she planned to paint cream. At least now she had a home. The only one she'd ever had, and filling it with people seemed to be the only way she would ever have the semblance of a family. She wouldn't be alone again. Not like all the years she'd spent in foster care. The half-dozen families she'd lived with, but never felt a part of. The only place she'd ever felt at home was here at Stewart Manor. That summer with her mother and Miss Hannah.

Tears filled her eyes. *Why did you leave me, Mom? Why couldn't you love me enough to keep me? Why couldn't someone love me?*

The sound of the doorbell caused Shelby to jump. Grabbing a tissue from the box on her desk, she went to answer the door and found the mailman on her porch.

"Ms. Harris?"

"That's me," she said.

He handed her an express-mail envelope and walked away.

"Thank you," she called, then closed the door and went back into the parlor. Tearing open the folder, she pulled out a short letter from her literary agent that said something to the effect that she should be pleasantly surprised with the royalty check included here, and that her editor was looking forward to her next book on Kellie Anne's adventures.

Shelby looked down at the amount of the check and nearly passed out. "Oh, my. I never realized," she murmured, staring at the large, five-figure amount. "This will certainly buy all the paint and wallpaper I need. And pay off a big debt to a certain contractor."

She thought about Rafe and all the things he'd done for her, never once asking for money. She couldn't let him continue his generosity. She grabbed her purse and headed for the door.

Around noon Rafe wiped the sweat from his forehead and eyed his work. Josh had helped him hang the drywall, but Rafe had done the mudding and taping himself.

"And a damn good job if I do say so myself," he murmured, rotating his sore shoulder.

"I'd say it looks great."

He turned around to find Shelby in the doorway. She made quite a picture in her short print skirt and cream-colored T-shirt with a denim vest.

"You look pretty."

She looked him over and smiled. "Thank you. You look…filthy."

"Does that mean I'm not going to get a kiss for my labor?"

She leaned forward and gave him a quick peck on the mouth, then brought out a bag of hamburgers from behind her back.

"How about we go downstairs and eat lunch? I have a surprise for you."

His pulse began to race. "Sure. I'll wash up so I won't leave any fingerprints on you," he said.

They made their way down to the kitchen where Rafe stripped off his T-shirt and stuck his head under the faucet. After washing away the dust from the drywall, he took the towel she handed him and dried off, then draped it around his neck. Before Shelby could step away, he grabbed her and pulled her into his arms. His mouth came down on hers. He'd been hungry for the taste of her all morning, but never knew how much until now. And when she pressed herself into him, it was almost too much.

He tore his mouth away. "You're a very tempting lady, *cara*."

She tried to step back, but he held her close. "Maybe we shouldn't be doing this," she said.

"Then you better just shoot me and put me out of my misery. Because I don't think I can be around you without touching you." He ran his finger down her arm and enjoyed her involuntary shiver.

Shelby pulled out of his embrace. "We should eat lunch before it gets cold."

He read the side of the brown bag. "From my favorite place, too." He was touched she'd driven across town.

"I had some errands to do and I was near the Pixie Diner. Besides, I have to keep you working," she teased, and popped a french fry in her mouth.

Rafe sat down at the counter as Shelby went to the refrigerator and poured two glasses of iced tea. She joined him, and during the meal they discussed the next step on the house. Rafe suggested he tackle replacing the spindles and the missing steps in the staircase, then refinishing the hardwood floors.

"Then I can paint and wallpaper?"

He loved her enthusiasm. "I've never met anyone so willing to work."

She smiled. "This is my home and I want it fixed up."

"So you can open it up during the fall festival?"

She took a bite of hamburger. After she swallowed, she said, "It would be good for business then, wouldn't it?"

Rafe was so busy watching her mouth he nearly missed

the question. "Uh, yeah. Could be," he said. "Not to worry, we have time to get things in shape."

"That's what I wanted to talk to you about. All the work you've been doing." She reached for her purse, took out an envelope and handed it to him.

He cocked an eyebrow.

She smiled. "Open it."

He tore open the envelope and pulled out a check. It was for the full amount of the quote he'd given her the day they met. His heart sank. "What's this?"

"It's the money I owe you."

He felt confused. Things had changed between them since then, hadn't they? Or was she trying to put things back on a business relationship? "Not this much. We worked out a deal, remember?"

"But you've done a lot more for me, Rafe. I couldn't let you give up your time when you could be making money elsewhere."

"What if I wanted to be here? What if I enjoyed doing things for you?" Damn, he wanted to be with her.

She hesitated, then finally spoke. "I told you before. I can't accept charity, Rafe."

He stood and forcefully pushed the stool back. "I wasn't giving you charity, Shelby. I was offering friendship." He tossed the check on the counter. "If you'd like to pay for the materials, fine. I'll send a bill, but all the rest was freely given." Before she could say anything, he grabbed his shirt and marched out.

By the time he'd made it to the truck, he was fuming even more. Dammit. Why did she keep pushing him away?

Well, the hell with stubborn women. Who needed them? He started the engine and backed out of the drive, then headed down the street, not knowing where his hurt pride would take him.

An hour later, after a drive around the lake, Rafe pulled

up at the construction office. He walked into the one-story building, past the reception desk where Angelina was talking on the phone. With a wave, Rafe continued on to his office, but didn't get the door closed before Angelina called after him.

"Just hold my calls," he shouted, and slammed his door.

Seconds later Angelina came barging in. "Hello to you, too."

Rafe sat down behind his desk. "Hello and goodbye." He pushed the pile of blueprints off to one side, then put his feet up on top.

She made her way across the room. "Boy, you sure got up on the wrong side of the bed, or maybe I should say *in* the wrong bed this morning."

He glared at her. "Don't push me, sis. I'm not in the mood."

"Oh, poor baby." She placed her hands on her hips. "You had a fight with Shelby and you blew it."

He dropped his feet to the floor and sat up straight. "How did you know we had—" He stopped. "We didn't fight."

"All right, what happened, then?" Angelina perched on a corner of the desk. "The last two days you've been happier than I've seen you in years. And after all the waves you two were making in the lake Sunday, I figured you were getting pretty…close. And this morning, when Shelby sent me our web-page design…"

Rafe frowned. "What web page?"

Angelina jumped off the desk. "Come with me." She led him to her computer in the outer office. "Shelby has designed a web page for Covelli and Sons."

His sister clicked the mouse and a colorful page with the Covelli and Sons logo appeared on the screen. It gave a description of the types of carpentry and construction jobs they did and how long they'd been in business. It was attractive and professionally done. He swallowed the big lump in his throat as he realized how much time and work Shelby had put into this page.

"This is advertising for the future." Angelina glanced over her shoulder. "Shelby planned to surprise you. Said you've done so much for her that she wanted the world to know what a great company we are."

Rafe felt like crawling into a hole.

Angelina clicked the button again. "She also did an ad for Maria's Ristorante." Then his sister showed him yet another page for their storefront offices under "Business Rentals."

Angelina glared at him. "Now, tell me what you did to blow it."

"Who blew what?"

They both turned to see that Tony and Rick had walked in. The last thing Rafe wanted to do was discuss his personal life with the family. "It's nothing. Shelby and I will work it out."

Tony smiled. "Hey, if you drop out of the picture, maybe I can have a chance with her."

"Over my dead body." Rafe turned and marched back to his office. He tried to shut the door, but Rick followed him in.

"So you and Shelby had your first fight," he said, and folded his arms.

"Oh, hell, it's closer to our tenth," Rafe confessed. "Every time I turn around we're arguing about something. Do you know what she did today?" Rafe moved around the room. "She paid me. She paid me for the work I've been doing on the house."

Rick shook his head and tried to hide a smile. "That's terrible. What was she thinking?"

Rafe sighed in exasperation. "Would you take money from Jill?"

Rick sobered. "I get your point," he said. "But I don't think Shelby realized you were doing all that work just for...her. Didn't you give her a bid initially?"

Rafe nodded. "Yeah, but later we made a sort of work-exchange deal. I'm doing her ceiling and she's teaching me...about computers. Then today, out of the blue, she gave me a check for the whole job. Everything."

"You were learning about computers?" Rick chuckled, then grew serious again. "Did you explain nicely that you couldn't take money for something you did out of love for her?"

Rafe opened his mouth to deny his brother's words. Instead, he groaned and ran his hands over his face. Good Lord, he'd fallen in love with her. His heart began to pound as he looked at Rick. "How did you know?"

"I'm familiar with the symptoms."

"What am I going to do?"

Rick smiled. "I suggest you take a deep, relaxing breath, call the florist and order flowers, then apologize to her for flying off the handle."

"Think that'll work?"

"Did with Jill."

There was a knock on the door and Angelina poked her head inside. "Rod Delany from Delany Construction is on line one."

Rafe blinked. Why was the biggest contractor in southern Indiana calling him? He picked up the receiver. "Hello, Mr. Delany."

"Hello, Rafe. And please call me Rod."

"What can I do for you, Rod?"

"If you're not too busy, I'd like for us to get together sometime this week. I have a proposition to discuss with you."

Delany Construction was well-known in the area. They'd built everything from shopping malls to housing tracts.

Rafe glanced at his desk calendar. "Sure, how about Thursday morning?"

"That's fine. Could you come to my office in Bedford?"

"No problem," Rafe said. He wrote down the address, then hung up the phone.

Rick cocked an eyebrow. "I'd say things are looking up if we're getting calls from Rod Delany."

Tony walked into the office. "What did he want?"

Rafe shrugged. "Tell you after I meet with him Thursday." Then he grinned and the three exchanged high fives. "You guys want to come along?"

"Sure," Tony said.

Rick raised a hand. "I think I'll hang back here and let you two handle things."

Angelina poked her head in the office again. "Our luck is changing," she said. "I'll tell Nonna her praying has paid off. Or maybe this article in the newspaper had something to do with it." She walked in and held up the morning paper.

Rafe grabbed it and read the headlines: PETER HARDIN CHARGED WITH MANSLAUGHTER. SUSPICIONS ABOUT CAVELLI MISCONDUCT CLEARED.

After Rafe left, Shelby didn't feel much like doing anything. His words had hurt. How could he think she didn't care about him? She wasn't any good at this. Everything she'd done for him seemed to be wrong.

She spent most of the day with Lucky curled up at her feet as she lay on her bed, reading Miss Hannah's diary. The diary was like a novel. Shelby tried to put it down several times, but found she couldn't stop reading. She couldn't stop wondering what was going to happen to the mistress of the manor.

When she'd gotten to the part where Hannah's parents insisted she give up her baby for adoption, Shelby had cried. Now, as she read how Hannah had fought them, she cheered, but in the end Hannah decided she had to do what was best for her child.

Hannah had gone to a home for unwed mothers, but after her little girl was born, she took the baby and ran away. But when she ran out of money, Hannah had to contact her parents again. Somehow she convinced her mother she would give up her baby, Susan Pauline, only if she could stay in touch with her child. Reluctantly her parents agreed and hired a lawyer to handle a private adoption. It took place in Indianapolis, and the Browns, the young couple who adopted her daughter, lived in Bedford and agreed to allow Hannah to visit regularly.

The first few years everything seemed fine. Then the day came when Hannah went to visit Susan—and her heart was broken.

April 17, 1947
Today I drove to Bedford to visit Susan, but when I arrived I found the Browns had moved away! The house was empty, and any trace of a family living there was gone, along with my child. I ran from neighbor to neighbor begging for information, but no one could tell me anything. It seems the Brown family has disappeared, including the only person who matters to me—my child.

Somehow I made it back to Haven Springs and told Mother what happened. She said it was for the best, that if someone discovered my secret, the family's good name would be ruined. Mother says I need to forget this time in my life.

How can I ever forget the child I gave life to, who grew inside me, whose father I'll love until my dying breath? I don't want to go on. Everyone that I loved is gone.

Sadness tore at Shelby's heart as she turned to the next entry, but all she found was a blank page. She turned another leaf to find the same. The rest of the book was completely blank.

No, there had to be more! Shelby had to find out what happened to Hannah and her little girl. She glanced overhead. Maybe in the attic.

She hurried out of her bedroom. Grabbing the keys off the hook and the flashlight from the drawer, she dashed up the stairs and along the hall. It was nearly dark, but that didn't deter Shelby. She wasn't afraid of being up there alone.

She opened the attic door and flicked on the light. Flashlight in hand, she headed up the steps to the attic, then to the secret room. After unlocking the door and turning on the light, Shelby went to the white chest and opened it. The cat beside her, she knelt down and searched through the things inside. There had to be another diary. Shelby dug through the baby clothes. This time when Shelby touched the tiny items, she knew they belonged to Susan Pauline. She carefully set the clothes down beside her. At last she found what appeared to be another diary under a baby blanket.

Shelby picked up the flashlight and opened the first page. She smiled when she found Hannah's name inside and the opening date of January 1, 1950. Shelby's hand froze on the page. Dear God. Hannah hadn't written in three years.

Shelby started to read when she heard her name being called. It was Rafe. She started putting everything back in the chest as she heard him coming up the steps to the second floor.

"I'm in the attic," she shouted.

Within seconds he was there. "I was worried when I couldn't find you. What are you doing up here?" he asked.

She wanted to be angry, but her heart tripped at the handsome man holding the bouquet of flowers. Dressed in khaki pants and a wine-colored shirt, his hair still damp from a shower, Rafe took her breath away.

Despite everything, she was happy to see him. But she couldn't stop herself from asking, "What are you doing here?"

He lost some of his attitude. "I came to apologize to you. I acted like a real jerk earlier."

"I'd say that was about right," she said, liking him a little humble. She doubted that Rafe Covelli admitted he'd been wrong very often.

"You think you can forgive me?" He held out the daisies.

Shelby was touched. No one had ever given her flowers before. She stood as he came closer.

Rafe wanted to pull Shelby into his arms. But after talking with Jill today, he resisted, knowing he had to earn Shelby's trust again. "I never should have refused your check."

Shelby glanced down at the flowers. "I'm going to pay you, Rafe. I've always paid my way."

He sighed. "I know. It just took me a while to understand. I should know better. You like to be independent, just as I do. You'd think I'd get the message having lived with three women. Can you forgive me?"

She nodded. But when he reached for her, she stepped back. "Maybe we should keep things businesslike—for a while."

His heart was breaking, but he kept remembering Jill's words: *Just give Shelby some space.* He backed off and glanced around the room. "Hey, what is this place? A secret hideout?"

Shelby shrugged. "Just a room."

"But, it's…a little girl's room." Rafe went to the dresser and examined the row of old dolls. "Do you think it was

Miss Hannah's playroom when she was a kid?'' When he glanced toward the closet, he felt Shelby tense, so he didn't go there. But it hurt that she didn't want to share this place with him.

"Probably," she said.

Rafe watched as Shelby knelt down next to the chest and began to put away some things. She seemed nervous, as if she'd been caught at something she shouldn't be doing.

She closed and locked the chest. "Why don't we go downstairs?" She picked up the flowers and a leather-bound book off the bed. Rafe grabbed the flashlight and followed her out.

Downstairs in the kitchen, Shelby offered him coffee. Rafe could tell she didn't want him to stay, so he declined. He pulled an envelope from his pocket. "Here's your new bill."

Shelby laid the flowers and the leather-bound book on the counter. Rafe had to admit he was curious as to what was inside. But he concentrated on Shelby as she opened the envelope.

"I adjusted some of the items," he began, "like the roof, since we didn't replace the whole thing, just patched it. I charged you for the drywall in the bedroom along with the labor to remove the old ceiling." He leaned closer, pointing to a line, and inhaled her sweet fragrance. "There's the amount I paid Josh and the boys last week for helping me. I'll be charging you for refinishing the floors and fixing the staircase, along with the window frames and woodwork in the front room. I also added twelve dollars to the bill for a year's rent for the rolltop desk that will be brought over as soon we finish the floors."

Their eyes met and he could barely find his voice. Her eyes were a shimmery sea-green, causing him to want things she wasn't ready to give him. Would she ever be?

"The bid seems fair," she said. "Can I write you a check?"

He nodded. "Half the amount is acceptable. I want to make sure you're satisfied with the remaining work before you pay in full. I'll send out a crew tomorrow to get started. If that's okay with you."

"I just want to know when you begin to sand the floors. I'll move out to the cottage."

"You can't stay there," he said, appalled. "That place hasn't been cleaned yet and several of the windows are broken. Look, I have an idea. Why not stay at my apartment?"

He saw the shock register on her face, then a cute rosy blush appeared. "No, I couldn't—"

"Wait," he interrupted. "I won't be there. I'll stay at Mom's. There's no problem with me moving back into my old room for a few days."

She looked doubtful. "You sure?"

"I'd feel better if you did. The cottage isn't in any shape to stay in."

They both looked down as Lucky strolled into the room. The little cat went over to Rafe, rubbed against his leg and purred. At least he was attractive to some females, Rafe thought. "You never know when you might run into another freeloader." He pulled out his key ring and handed her a key. "I'll be out of town on Thursday. Why don't you move over then?"

She nodded shyly. Rafe hated that she was acting nervous again. Give her space, he kept repeating to himself. Don't push too hard. But that was exactly what he wanted to do. He wanted to take her in his arms and kiss her until she realized how much she cared for him. But he wasn't going to do that, at least not tonight. "Well, I'd better be off." He turned away, disappointed.

"Wait. I have to pay you." She rushed to her purse and pulled out her checkbook.

"You don't need to give it to me now," he said.

She kept writing. "I got that check I've been expecting. And I'm going to order my paint and wallpaper tomorrow."

"I'll go with you so Ben Clark will give you a discount."

Shelby shook her head as she handed him the check. "I can't let you take time away from your day."

He didn't look at it, just slipped it into his shirt pocket. "It's not going to take the whole day. Besides, you're a paying client. I do it all the time. I don't want you to overpay."

She smiled at him and his pulse raced. "Okay, if it's not too much trouble, I'd appreciate your coming along."

"Anytime, say, about twelve?"

She nodded. "And thank you for allowing me to stay in your apartment."

The thought of Shelby in his bed stirred up a lot of wild fantasies. "No problem." He stepped closer, determined he wasn't leaving until he got a kiss. "Just helping out a friend. Will we continue working together on the computer?"

She shrugged. "I guess so. I'll have my laptop with me."

Her soft voice shot warmth through him. "I want to thank you for the web page you did for Covelli and Sons. You're very good." He wanted her so much, he couldn't get his feet to move.

"Thank you. I'm glad you liked it."

"I did. Again, I'm sorry about how I acted this morning. I'll try and curb my—as Angelina calls it—caveman tactics."

She smiled. "I can be a little stubborn, too."

"We seem to throw off sparks when we're together.

That's what I like about you. You give as good as you get." He stepped closer and slipped his arm around her waist. She didn't resist.

"Where I came from, you had to."

"I had to, too," he said. "But I hate arguing with you." He lowered his head, and when she didn't pull away, his mouth closed over hers. A hot rush of desire raced through him, but he fought to hold it in check. He kept his kiss sweet and light. Finally he pulled away.

His eyes locked with hers and he saw the longing there.

"I'd better go. See you tomorrow," he finally managed.

He turned and walked out the back door, knowing there was no way he'd get any sleep tonight. Not when he'd be thinking about Shelby and how he was going to convince her they belonged together.

Chapter Ten

On Thursday morning, carrying her suitcase and laptop, Shelby made her way up the stairs to Rafe's apartment. She set her things down, dug through her shoulder bag and pulled out the key Rafe had given her. With a calming sigh, she unlocked the door and stepped inside. She placed her computer on the kitchen table and carried the suitcase into the bedroom. She froze as she eyed the queen-size bed, covered with a navy blue comforter.

There seemed to be a big neon sign on the headboard that read Rafe Sleeps Here. The vivid picture of his large body tangled in white sheets, his broad chest naked except for the mat of dark hair that ran over his flat stomach and disappeared under the sheet caused her to gasp. Shelby pushed the wayward thought out of her head. She had to stop thinking about Rafe.

Opening her suitcase, she took out a makeup bag and went into the bathroom. The entire room sparkled with chrome fixtures and a black-and-white-tiled floor. She opened the bag and set her things on the counter. There was a single toothbrush hanging in the holder, and a place beside it for another one. She gripped hers in her hand and decided not to get too comfortable. This was only a short stay. Years in foster care had caused her to adopt the motto Always Be Ready to Leave. She zipped up the bag and pushed it into the corner.

A sudden knock on the door drew her attention and she went to answer it. Jill stood in the hall holding two sacks of groceries. "I was hoping to get here before you arrived."

"Aren't I supposed to be here yet?"

Smiling, Jill walked inside. "Of course, but I wanted a chance to stock the cupboards. I have a feeling that Rafe doesn't have much in the way of food. He eats at the restaurant most of the time." She set the groceries on the table, opened the refrigerator and eyed the meager contents—a six-pack of beer and a carton of orange juice. "I was right. Well, it's a good thing I brought some staples."

Shelby watched as Jill pulled out a loaf of bread, canned soup, some lettuce, tomatoes and lunch meat. "You're not required to feed me, you know. Rafe was nice enough, lending me his apartment."

"Rafe's a nice guy. He's only making sure you're taken care of."

Shelby looked away. "I'm not used to that."

Jill sat down at the table and motioned for Shelby to join her. "I'm afraid that comes with the Covelli men. They have this strong urge to take care of their women." Another smile appeared on her face. "When I first met Rick, every time I turned around he seemed to be there wanting to help me with something. It was like I didn't have a chance to be independent or just be alone. One day I told him to stay away, and when he did I missed him so much I thought I'd go crazy." Jill's gaze met Shelby's. "One thing about the Covelli men, when they love, they don't do it halfway. It's forever."

Shelby knew Jill was trying to read her intentions. "I don't know if I'm the person Rafe needs in his life. I'm not good at relationships."

"I was the same way," Jill said. "The only other man I'd ever dated was Lucas's father, and he left me pretty bitter for a long time. But Rick saw through all of it and somehow pushed his way into my heart. I never thought I could love a man the way I love Rick. Body and soul."

Surprisingly Shelby found she envied Jill's relationship with Rick. But Shelby knew she could never give to a man like that. She'd learned from an early age never to trust anyone.

"Do you have feelings for Rafe?"

Shelby was taken aback by the bold question. "Yes, but I'm not sure I can trust...him or any man."

Jill's hand rested on hers. "Then take it slow. If it's meant to be, it'll happen."

"That's just it—I'm not sure I can let it happen. And the last thing I want to do is hurt Rafe."

Rafe and Tony didn't return from Bedford and their meeting with Rod Delany until four o'clock. They walked into the office and were greeted by Rick and Angelina.

"So tell us what happened," Angelina said.

"Let's go into the conference room first," Rafe suggested, and led the way.

"Okay, spill it," Rick said as he pulled out a chair at the table and sat down. "Before I choke it out of you."

Rafe looked at Tony, then back at his two siblings. His face split into a huge grin. "Looks like we're going to be pretty busy for a while. Rod Delany just offered Covelli and Sons all the carpentry work on a tract of homes he's building outside Bedford."

"Oh, my gosh!" Angelina gasped. "I read about that in the paper. There are two phases to this project. Phase one has already broken ground and Delany is going to build twenty-eight custom homes. Next spring there're another thirty-five tract homes to be built near the new electronics plant. If we get the job, that means…'' Her blue eyes widened. "Do you have any idea how much money this will bring in?"

Tony laid the folder he'd been carrying on the table.

"We crunched some numbers today, but we'll put together the finished bid by next week. Delany wants us to do all the custom woodworking and kitchen cabinets. Although we haven't talked about phase two, I believe Covelli and Sons is officially back on its feet."

The entire family cheered. Angelina ran into the outer office and came back carrying a bottle of wine and four glasses. She poured everyone a short drink and handed them out. "To the Covellis. We hung together and we made it," she said, then looked at Rafe. "I'm so proud of you for hanging in there when it would have been so easy to give up."

Rafe glanced up at the photograph on the wall of him standing beside his father. It was the day Rafe officially came into the business. He raised his glass. "To Dad, for teaching us the importance of family. *Salute!*"

"*Salute!*" everyone answered.

Rick threw his arm across Rafe's back. "I think you should take Dad's words to heart and go after some family happiness of your own."

Rafe's heartbeat accelerated. For the first time in a long time, he felt as if a weight had been lifted from his shoulders. He had a future, something to offer Shelby. But did she want it? Did she want *him*? Well, he sure as hell was going to find out.

Rafe called Shelby at his apartment and told her the good news, inviting her to join the family at the restaurant for a small celebration. When Shelby walked through the door at Maria's Ristorante, she found the place filled with people laughing and singing along to an Italian song. She watched the Covelli family interact as Rick, Rafe, Angelina and Jill hugged each other. Maria and Vittoria were greeting friends and patrons who had heard the news and come to help celebrate.

She felt like an outsider.

Rafe looked up and spotted her. She was dressed in a black print sundress that showed off her legs. Her feet were encased in sandals, exposing bright red toenails. Dark curls adorned her pretty face. Damn, she sure could make a man take notice.

He marched across the room and kissed her before she could protest. "Glad you made it."

"I really can't stay long. I have work to finish up."

"You need to eat," he argued. "Mom and Nonna will be upset if you don't have something to eat. Besides, I know there wasn't any food in my apartment." He pulled her close to his side and they went off to join the family.

"Shelby!" Maria cried. "You came to celebrate with us."

Vittoria stepped in. "And I'm such a proud *nonna*. I always have faith in my grandchildren. The curse will never destroy the Covelli family."

Rafe bent down so his grandmother could kiss his cheeks. Then Vittoria tugged Shelby down to kiss her, too.

After a while, Shelby relaxed as she ate with the family. Rafe introduced her to many of the patrons. Conversation was comfortable, as the main topic was the fall festival. Her neighbor, Rose Kerrigan, gave suggestions on where to shop for furniture for the house.

Finally Rafe managed to tear Shelby away from the others and walk her back to the apartment, barely two blocks from the restaurant. Climbing up the stairs, he was quiet, not needing words as much as her closeness. He was hungry for the feel and smell of her skin, for her warmth.

They got to the door and he unlocked it. It was strange knowing she was staying in his apartment and he wasn't there with her. Would he ever climb into bed again without aching for her?

"I had fun tonight," she said.

"Not as much as I did." Rafe closed the door and backed her against it. "But I'm going to have more as soon as I kiss you properly." He bent his head toward her, then hesitated as her lips parted in anticipation. "Unless you'd rather I didn't kiss you." He teased her by sliding his tongue along her lower lip. She gasped. "Tell me, *cara.* Tell me how much you want me to kiss you." His tongue stole across her mouth again and she whimpered. "Maybe I should show you how much I want you."

He took her hand and placed it under his shirt against his heart. "Feel how hard it's pounding? How much you excite me?"

She closed her eyes and leaned her head back against the door. "Oh, Rafe."

He released her hand, but she didn't take it away; instead, she found his nipple and ran her nail over the tip until it hardened. He groaned, then took her mouth in a hungry kiss.

Her arms came around his neck as he pressed his body against hers and he drank eagerly from her sweetness. He couldn't get enough. His hands moved to her dress. Finding the buttons, he worked to get them open. Finally he was able to reach inside and caress her breasts, and she whimpered in pleasure. He knew the next step was his bed.

"I want you, *cara.*" His head rested against hers as they held each other, both trembling. "Like no other woman I've ever known. But I have to walk out this door so we can both wake up tomorrow without regrets."

She nodded.

With the last of his sanity, he kissed the tip of her nose and walked out the door, wondering if she was going to love him...or hate him.

The following Monday morning Rafe walked up the steps of Stewart Manor. This was the first time he would be seeing Shelby since he left her at his apartment. He had no idea if she would ever speak to him again, but he wasn't going to give up. He knew she cared about him. And he was tired of being patient.

"Rafe," she said as she opened the cut-glass-paneled door.

"I wanted to stop by and see if you liked how the floors turned out." He stepped inside the entry and glanced down at the shining honey-colored floors. He'd spent his weekend here to get the job done so Shelby could move back home. His job at this house was finished and they could move on to a personal relationship.

"They're beautiful. Didn't Charlie tell you I thought you did a wonderful job?"

"How about the windows and woodwork?"

"I can't believe the woodwork is anything but the original. It's perfect." She walked into the front room. "I've ordered new curtains for the windows, but I hate to hide the beautiful wood."

She seemed more interested in the windows than in him. "How about upstairs? Everything the way you want?" he asked.

"No problems. Ben Clark gave me the name of a wallpaper hanger. He's coming tomorrow to start on the bedrooms."

"I thought you were going to hang it. I was planning on helping."

She sighed. "I don't want you to do any more, Rafe. I owe you so much already."

"And I told you I want to help. Why won't you let me?"

She looked frustrated. "Because I just can't."

"I thought we were friends, Shelby. And friends help each other."

She crossed the room. "I'm sorry Rafe. This time you're not going to get your way. You won't change my mind."

"You think I'm doing this for my ego?" he asked. "Hell, I could go climb a mountain for that. I want to be with you, Shelby. I care about you. I think you care about me, too. In fact, we both know we're more than just friends."

"I can't!" she exclaimed. "I knew this would happen. I knew if you got close that..." She paused.

"That we'd fall in love."

Her eyes widened and she shook her head. "No! I'm the wrong person for you."

"What are you so frightened of?"

She glanced around like a cornered animal, looking for a way out. "I don't know how to...feel."

"I know how I feel. And I think deep down, so do you." He started across the room, but when she raised a hand, he stopped.

"You don't even know me," she said. "Not the real me."

"I know all I need to know."

"Do you know that I've been lying to you since the moment we met?"

Rafe froze, watching as she walked to the mantel. "See all these pictures? Well, they aren't my relatives. In fact, I don't even know who these people are. The pictures came with the frames when I bought them at garage sales." Shelby hugged herself. He could see her trembling.

"It was an accident at first," she continued. "I never

planned to make up a family—it just happened when some-one asked about the people in the pictures. It was so easy to do, instead of explaining that no one...wanted me." She looked at him and her eyes filled with tears. "It doesn't hurt so much that way. And you don't get all those pitying looks."

Rafe swallowed back his own emotions, wanting des-perately to go to her. "What did happen to your parents?"

She shrugged. "My father didn't stick around. Mom did for a while, but ended up giving me away when I was six."

Rafe clenched his fists. How could anyone abandon a child?

"Nola Harris preferred having a man in her life to having her child. I went into foster care then. A few years later, I heard she'd died of a drug overdose." Shelby's gaze met his and he saw the years of loneliness etched on her face.

"You want to know why I bought this big old house? It was because my mother and I lived here one summer. I think she must have worked for the Stewart family. We stayed in the cottage out back. It was the best time I ever had. Miss Hannah was so nice to me." Shelby's voice cracked. "Then one day, there was a fight between my mother and Miss Hannah. We had to leave."

Shelby scrubbed at the tears on her cheeks. "But all those years I was in foster homes, I thought about my sum-mer here and the nice lady who gave me strawberry ice cream and read me stories. The simple kindness of Miss Hannah made this place feel like the only home I've ever had."

Rafe didn't wait for permission. He crossed the room swiftly and took her in his arms. At first she fought him, but he continued to hold her. And then she began to cry.

"Shh, *cara*, I'm here. I'll always be here for you." He never realized how much he meant the words, or how much he loved Shelby until this moment.

After a while Shelby's crying stopped. She'd gathered her composure, but that didn't erase the fact that she'd just told Rafe her whole sordid life story.

She pushed him away. "I'm sorry. I don't usually do that."

"There's nothing wrong with showing your feelings," Rafe insisted. "I'm honored that you feel comfortable enough with me to share them."

She glanced away. "You didn't give me much choice. You have the stubbornness of a pit bull."

"If that's what it takes, I'm glad I do. I want to help."

Shelby didn't want his help, or his pity. Why couldn't he leave her alone? She didn't like the feelings he caused in her. "I think I'm a lost cause."

"You're not. Let me help you, Shelby. I lov—"

She stopped his words with her finger against his mouth. "Please Rafe, I'm not ready. I don't know if I'll ever be ready to trust enough to..."

He nodded, but she could see the pain she caused him. Worse, she was selfish enough to want to curl up in his arms and take all that he had to offer. But he deserved better.

"How about for now we start out as friends?" Rafe suggested. He wrapped his hand around her fingers, brought them to his mouth and placed a kiss on the tips.

Shelby felt the jolt of heat all the way to her toes. "I thought you said that was like a kiss-off."

"I said we'll start there, but that doesn't mean that's all we'll ever be." He wiggled his dark eyebrows. "I can be a pretty persuasive guy."

Over the next week Shelby painted and papered the bedrooms. And no matter how much she argued, Rafe was right beside her, saying he had to make sure that nothing got on the newly refinished floors.

On Saturday they'd gone shopping with Rick and Jill at an antique flea market where she purchased a beautiful secretary desk and a set of china. Later they stopped for lunch at a coffee shop in Bedford and sat in a booth by the window.

"You know there's an estate sale this week at the McCaffey House," Jill said. "You might be able to find some more dishes, and maybe a sofa and some chairs. Maria said that Margaret McCaffey used to entertain a lot before she got sick."

"What I really need is to find rugs for downstairs."

"To cover my floors," Rafe said, acting wounded.

"Just area rugs," she said, giving him a sideways glance to see his smile. "There'll be plenty of floor showing."

"It's a good thing. I worked long and hard so those floors would shine." Rafe put his arm around her shoulders and pulled her close. She was so used to his touch that it felt natural. But when she glanced across the booth, Jill and Rafe were staring curiously at them. Shelby quickly sat up a little straighter.

"Jill, do you think that estate sale will have some rugs?"

"Probably. I hear that everything in the house is to be sold. You want to go together?"

"That would be great."

Rick looked at his wife. "Want me to go, too, or just hand over the checkbook?"

"Checkbook, and I'll call if I need you to bring the truck."

Rick groaned. "Maybe I should just head back to Texas and start drilling another well. This old house of ours is costing a small fortune to redo."

"It'll be worth it when it's finished," Jill said as she snuggled closer to her husband. "And speaking of finishing, you need to get busy on one room especially." The couple exchanged a look that made Shelby blush.

"Should we tell them?" Rick said to his wife. Jill nodded.

Rick grinned. "It looks like we're going to be adding to the family. Jill's pregnant."

There was a shout of joy from Rafe. Shelby opened her mouth to speak, but no words came. She'd never considered having children herself, but suddenly she couldn't escape the thought of carrying Rafe's baby.

Rafe stood and pulled his brother into an embrace. "That's great, bro," he said. "When? Have you told Mom?" He kissed Jill.

"Whoa. One at a time. The baby is due in March. And keep the news to yourself. We're going to tell Mom and Nonna as soon as we get back today and pick up Lucas."

Rafe was still smiling. "I can't believe it. Another Covelli. Ain't love grand?"

"Maybe you should try it," Rick said. "I never knew how wonderful life could be until I met Jill."

Shelby wanted to crawl under the table. Was she the one who was keeping Rafe from finding love and marriage?

When they arrived home thirty minutes later, Rick and Rafe carried in her desk and put it in the entry. Along with the deacon's bench under the stairs, the room was beginning to fill up nicely.

Shelby took Jill upstairs to show her the new wallpaper. The master suite was the closest to being finished. The pink-and-green floral paper had been hung this week. The bed was covered with a deep-rose satin comforter and matching dust ruffle. The window seat had hunter green and rose pillows scattered across the surface. The country-scene pictures from the attic were now hanging on the walls.

The front bedroom where Rafe had redone the ceiling had been papered in a blue-and-white stripe. The iron bed from the attic had been painted a white enamel, and she'd added a new mattress and a white comforter. Shelby was proud of what she'd accomplished in the house, but there was a lot more to do.

She thanked Jill and Rick for a nice day. Rafe walked with her to the door as if he was living in the house, too. The thought thrilled Shelby. It was like one of those little-girl fantasies having your own knight in shining armor come and rescue you. But she'd never been rescued, and she'd given up such fantasies a long time ago.

Rafe took her in his arms and kissed her. She was the first to pull away. "It was a great day, but I need to get some work done tonight."

"I guess I'm being thrown out," Rafe said. Pain flashed across his face.

"You'd think you'd get tried of spending so much time here."

He looked at her, his expression vulnerable. "I would never tire of you. I just hope one day you'll believe me. Not all men use women. My grandfather and grandmother were very much in love, as were my parents. I would never intentionally hurt you, Shelby." He kissed her again, offering her his desire, proving her need for him.

"Oh, Rafe, I care about you, too. I'm just afraid."

He held her tight, pressing her head against his chest. "Don't ever be afraid to love me. I'll cherish you… forever."

Later that night Shelby felt restless. She couldn't sleep, thinking about Rafe and his promises. She picked up Miss Hannah's diary and began to read. Every night Shelby had been caught up in the ongoing story, the sad life of Hannah Stewart. How she become a prisoner in this house, taking care of her ailing mother after her father died. It was as if her rose garden was the only escape she had. But over the years Hannah still hoped she'd find her child, and she never stopped searching. Even after twenty years had passed, she'd kept on.

The passage Shelby read tonight revealed that Hannah had finally found her, Susan Pauline Brown. But that hadn't been her name for a long time. The Browns had changed it so that Hannah couldn't find them. They had wanted the child all to themselves. Susan's name was now Nola.

Shelby gasped. Her heart lodged in her throat as she reread the name. Nola. Her mother's name. With trembling fingers, Shelby turned the page, afraid to find the answer, but desperately needing to know the truth.

June 18, 1976
She finally arrived in Haven Springs today. My Susan. I was so afraid she would hate me. But she smiled. Such a pretty smile. Susan looks like her father. Tall and slender with his dark hair. Our meeting was awkward at first, especially since I could only meet her in the cottage, away from Mother. But Susan, I mean Nola, didn't seem to mind, nor did her little girl, Shelby.

I can't believe I have my baby with me at last.

June 24, 1976
Mother is beginning to suspect something is going on. She questioned me today about the people staying in the cottage. I told her that they're a friend's daughter and granddaughter. I don't think she believes me. But no matter what Mother says, I will not give Nola up, not this time.

July, 1, 1976
My heart is broken. Nola said she wants to stay, but needs money. A lot of money. I don't have much. Mother still controls the finances and she'll never let

me have it, especially for my secret child.

When I told Nola I couldn't give her any money, she got angry. Said she needs to buy medicine, but I know it was illegal drugs. When I told her no again, she threatened to leave. I promised I would get her some help, but she packed her bags and walked out dragging sweet Shelby, kicking and screaming.

Consumed by anger, Shelby tossed the diary across the room. "Why couldn't you have kept me, Hannah. Why?" All this time and she had a grandmother. Oh, God. Shelby got up and paced the floor, trying to comprehend what she'd read in the diary. She hugged herself as a sob tore from her throat. A family. She had a family. And even *they* hadn't wanted her. Nobody wanted her. She dug her fingernails into her arms, but she didn't feel the pain. Her heart was shattered.

Shelby jumped at the sound of a knock on the back door. Whoever it was, she wasn't in the mood to see anyone. The knock grew louder, and then she heard Rafe call her name.

She dried her eyes and went to the door. She opened it only slightly. "Rafe, I'm not in the mood for company tonight."

He disregarded her wishes and pushed past her. "I shouldn't have left you earlier, Shelby. We need to work this out."

She sighed. She couldn't do this now. "Rafe...stop. I've tried to tell you that there isn't anything to work out. I can't give you what you need." She fought for composure. "Please...just leave."

He looked like she'd struck him. Then his expression stiffened. "You can't mean that."

She bit her lower lip. Please just leave, she prayed silently.

He stepped closer, his brown eyes shimmering with pain.

"We both know you're lying, *cara*. You care about me. I got into your heart just as you got into mine."

She shook her head.

He drew a ragged breath. "Well, I hope you can live with yourself for throwing our love away."

She fought for strength as she let him walk out the door. She managed to shut it. When she heard his truck start, she began to cry. Tears poured down her face for the child that was never loved. And for sending the best man in the world out of her life. But in the end, he would leave her. Everyone always did.

Chapter Eleven

The pain tore at Rafe's gut. Not since his father's death had he felt so empty, so alone. It was as if his whole world was falling apart and there was nothing he could do to stop it.

He grabbed the wine bottle from the kitchen counter and slipped out the back door to his grandmother's garden. In the darkness, he found his way to the bench. He needed to escape his family's questions, questions he had no answers to.

God, it hurt. He'd offered his love and Shelby had tossed it back in his face.

"So this is where you ended up."

Rafe looked up to see his brother coming toward him. *I don't need this,* he thought. "Don't you have a wife to go home to?" Rafe took a long drink from the bottle, hoping the numbness would take over soon.

Rick handed him a glass. "Here, I'll join you." He sat down on the bench across from his brother and grabbed the chianti, then poured them both a glass. "Let's make a toast. To women—can't live without them, nor do we want to."

Rafe watched as Rick took a long swallow.

"Hey, come on, drink up, bro." He smiled. "We have a bottle to empty."

"What are you trying to do?" Rafe asked.

"Keep you company in your misery."

Rafe stood. "Well, stop it. I don't like it."

"Hey, I thought you wanted someone to feel sorry for you."

"Go to hell."

Rick's smile faded. "I've been there, too, bro. When Jill pushed me out of her life."

"Well, you've got her now, so you have nothin' to complain about."

"But if I'd given up on her and decided to get drunk, Jill wouldn't have become my wife."

Rafe took a swallow of wine. "Is this leading somewhere?"

"You know Shelby loves you, right?" Rick waved his hand. "Silly question. She looks at you like you've hung the moon."

Rafe swallowed. "She does?"

Rick nodded. "I noticed it the first time I went to work at her house. Her eyes followed your every move."

Rafe's pulse began to pound. "Then why did she tell me to get out of her life?"

His brother shrugged. "I'm not sure. But that's something you're going to have to find out." He took a sip of wine. "Unless you want to give up."

Rafe started to pace, knowing that everyone in Shelby's past had left her. He wasn't going to be added to that list. "Like hell. I just need to figure out what happened. We were getting so close, then she pulled back. I mean, she's told me things…'' Rafe stopped, not wanting to break her trust.

"Then go to her. Somehow convince her you aren't going to walk away like the others. That you'll be there no matter what.''

Rafe was doubtful. "That's all?''

"Probably not,'' Rick admitted. "If Shelby is anything like Jill, it'll take more to convince her. But I believe you've got enough staying power to wait it out.''

"Is this a test?''

Rick shook his head. "No. I believe Shelby has been hurt before, so she doesn't trust easily.'' He looked at his brother. "Give her reason to trust you.''

With renewed hope, Rafe handed his glass to his brother. "Thanks, bro. I'm gonna do my best.'' He had no choice because he couldn't give her up.

"And remember what Nonna always says—that if it's true love, nothing, not even the curse, will keep you apart.''

Rafe grinned. "I've never argued with Nonna before and I'm not about to start now.''

It wasn't until the next morning that Rafe made it to Shelby's house. But when he got there, she wasn't anywhere to be found. Fear raced through him. Had she gone back to Louisville? Well, he'd just go after her. Somehow he'd find her. He stepped off the back porch and saw Ely Cullen working in the garden.

Rafe walked out to meet him. The old man smiled as he approached. "Good morning, Rafe.''

"Morning, Ely. I've been meaning to tell you what a wonderful job you've done shaping up the grounds.'' Rafe glanced around at the pruned trees, the clipped hedges. The lawn had been manicured to perfection. He looked back at the old man. "Have you been careful not to work too hard?"

The gardener nodded. "My grandson takes care of me and so does Miss Shelby. If it gets too hot, she makes me stop or come inside."

That sounded like Shelby, Rafe thought. But who was around to make sure *she* didn't overdo? Well, he was. Or, at least he wanted to be. "Shelby also works too hard."

"That she does, but she's so excited about the house." Ely's smile faded. "But today she seems down, almost sad." He looked up at Rafe with a questioning expression. "That's not like her."

Rafe nodded. "I know, Ely. And you know I care about Shelby. A lot."

The old man grinned. "She's a special woman."

"Yes, she is. And something has been bothering her the last couple of days."

Ely glanced away. "It's been a rough job trying to get this place restored."

"It's more than that, Ely. You and I both know it. If there is anything you can tell me, to help me… I mean, it would never go any farther than us."

The gardener looked as if he was struggling with a decision. Finally he pushed back his battered straw hat and said, "She's been going through some of Miss Hannah's things. Her diary. In the afternoons, she usually reads for a while on the patio."

Rafe recalled the leather-bound book Shelby had brought down from the attic last week. "Is the book leather?"

The gardener nodded. "Yes. Years ago, I remember Miss Hannah sitting out on the side porch in the afternoon and writing in it. You think that has something to do with Miss Shelby being so sad lately?"

"I'm sure going to find out." Rafe's spirits lifted. At least he had a start. "Thanks Ely. Where's Shelby now?"

"She went into the cottage early this morning. I haven't seen her since."

"Did she have that book with her?"

"Not sure. She was carrying a basket of cleaning supplies. Said she was going to have a guy come by and give an estimate on replacing the broken windows."

Good, Rafe thought. At least Shelby wasn't planning on leaving town. If only he could get hold of that diary. It might be the key to what was going on with her.

He headed down the path to the cottage. When he reached the weathered building, he was careful to avoid the rotting wood on the porch, making a mental note to replace it; then he moved to the front door and went inside. He found the furniture pushed together and covered with sheets. The walls were void of pictures. It looked as if she was ready to paint. In the kitchenette he saw that the cupboards had been washed and the shelves relined. The old sink was scrubbed until it shined along with the tiled counters. But Rafe's interest was drawn to the leather-bound book on the table. Picking it up, he realized he wasn't alone. He turned and found Shelby in the bedroom doorway.

She wore a pair of washed-out jeans and an oversize T-shirt. A red bandanna covered her hair, but some wayward curls had escaped. Her pale complexion and the circles under her eyes suggested she hadn't slept any better than he had.

"Decided to clean the place up?"

"One thing you learn from being in foster homes is how to clean," she said. "I got so good at it I ran a cleaning service in college. What are you doing here?"

"I came by to check the staircase."

"I thought you finished everything last week."

Shelby's gaze went to Rafe's handsome face. His chocolate-brown eyes were like a magnet—how easily they drew her in. His perfectly shaped mouth brought back vivid memories of heated kisses. A jolt of awareness went through her, and she forced herself to look away. "Your trip wasn't necessary. Everything is fine."

"It's necessary for me. I just need to check the stairs I replaced," he insisted.

"What exactly do you need to look at?" Another rush of heat crept up her neck as Shelby couldn't resist a look of her own. At Rafe's worn jeans, which always seem to fit just right. At his T-shirt, which didn't disguise his musculature. Her blood surged as she recalled the feel of his broad chest, the comforting embrace of his arms... She shook away the thoughts, but not Rafe's amused expression when he caught her staring.

"I want to make sure the steps are nailed down," he said, then he looked at the diary on the table. He picked it up. "This Miss Hannah's diary?"

Panic raced through Shelby. The last thing she wanted was him looking through that. "What makes you think it's a diary?"

"Ely told me that Hannah used to write in a brown leather book." He held it up. "I think this is the same one. Were you reading this last night when you decided we weren't meant to be together?"

She crossed to him and took the diary from his hand. "It's not any business of yours what I read. Is it wrong to be curious about the woman whose house I lived in?" She gripped the book tightly. "Beside, it doesn't matter anymore. I stopped reading."

"Why, Shelby?"

She shrugged. "I have too many other things to do than

spend my free time reading an old diary. Right now, I have to go into town and pick up something from the hardware store. I need to fix the bathroom sink.''

"I could look at it for you."

"Always Rafe to the rescue. Thanks, but I think I'd better get used to doing things for myself." She saw his hurt look and felt like a heel.

"Fine, do it yourself. Then you won't mind if I read a little about Miss Hannah. As you know, I was a history major in college, so I should find it interesting." He reached for the book.

Shelby held on to it. "I don't think Hannah's personal thoughts should be passed around." She started to walk away, but Rafe grabbed her arm and stopped her.

"What are you afraid I'll find out if I read the diary?"

"Nothing," she denied, but couldn't control her trembling.

"Is it so hard to trust me, Shelby?" he asked, pain etched around his eyes. "What did I do that was so terrible you can't stand the sight of me? Doesn't a condemned man deserve to know what he's accused of?"

"It's not you, Rafe. It's me. There are things in the diary…" She stole a look at him and saw his confusion. "Please, I can't." Shelby felt the tears threaten, but couldn't do anything to stop them. "Okay, you want to know the truth? Here." She shoved the diary into his hand. "But to get the whole story you need to start with Hannah's first diary. It's in the chest in that room in the attic. The key is on the hook in the kitchen." She tried to leave, but Rafe took hold of her arm.

"No matter what I read, Shelby, it isn't going to change anything. I love you."

She wanted desperately to believe him, but she couldn't

handle being abandoned again. "Oh, Rafe," she breathed. "You can't—"

"The hell I can't," he said. "I've lain awake night after night wanting you, aching for you—and not for the moment, Shelby, *forever*." He shut his eyes and drew a calming breath. "But if you can tell me you don't feel the same, then I'll walk away."

Shelby closed her eyes against the constricting pain in her chest. They both knew she couldn't say it. Somehow she managed to break his hold and she ran off toward the house. She couldn't stay with Rafe here. Besides, after he read Hannah's story and discovered the shame she would bring to Haven Springs's founding family, he wouldn't want her anymore.

After Shelby took off, Rafe walked up to the house, determined to find out everything. He passed through the kitchen and grabbed the ring of keys off the hook. He continued into the entry and took the steps two at a time, then hurried down the long hall to the attic door. He unlocked it and went up the narrow stairs. Without hesitation he covered the distance to the locked room and worked the key until the lock gave way. Inside, he flicked on the light. He spotted the chest and lifted the lid. There, on top of a blanket, was another leather-bound book.

He picked it up and opened it. On the first page, he saw the date and couldn't believe it. He began leafing through the yellowed pages, knowing he couldn't possibly get through the whole book before Shelby returned. But he had to try to find the reason for her pain. He wasn't about to let her slip out of his life.

He got to the part where Miss Hannah had fallen in love with a man, Paul Braden, who was later killed in World War II. A month after his death she'd discovered she was pregnant with his child. "My, oh, my, Miss Hannah," he murmured. "You did have a secret."

"That's not the only one."

Rafe looked up and saw Shelby in the doorway. He stood. Why did he feel like he'd been caught doing something wrong? She said he could read the damn journal.

She came inside. "I guess I shouldn't be surprised you're here."

"I needed to find out what made you change your mind about…us."

Several emotions flashed across her face. "There never was any *us*, Rafe," she said. "From the beginning, I told you there never could be."

"There could if you'd let me in. Let me help you, Shelby. Trust me enough to let my love shield you from whatever is hurting you. Whatever it is."

She didn't say anything.

He went to her, seeing the years of loneliness in her luminous green eyes. "I love you, Shelby. I think I have since the first time I saw you standing on the porch."

She closed her eyes, but there was a lifetime of pain etched on her face. Pain he wanted to kiss away.

"Shelby, I know no matter how hard I try, I can never know the rough life you had growing up. Or never know what it was like not having a family. But if you'll let me, I'll be your family."

Her eyes opened and filled with tears, and her lips trembled as she began to speak. "That's the worst part. I've always had a family. But I never knew it. Never was part of it."

"Where?"

She nodded at the second diary. "It's in there. I'm a Stewart. Miss Hannah was my grandmother."

Rafe nearly smiled in relief, but realized that Shelby

didn't share his relief. "Let me get this straight. Your mother was the baby Hannah gave up?"

Shelby nodded. "The second generation's secret baby. No one wanted me, either. Not my mother, not even my grandmother."

"Shelby, you don't know you weren't wanted. Your grandmother loved your mother. She had to love and want you just as much." He reached for her and managed to pull her into his arms. He closed his eyes, savoring the feel of her body against his.

He leaned back and raised her chin with his finger. He had to get through to her. "I need you in my life, Shelby. I need you more than my next breath."

Tears ran down her cheeks. "Please, Rafe. If you care about me, you won't make this any harder. How would Haven Springs feel about the daughter of the illegitimate child of a founding family? I can't go through that. I've decided to put the house up for sale. I'm moving back to Louisville." She pulled away and walked out.

Rafe's chest ached. Shelby was slipping away and nothing he could do or say would stop her. "Dammit, Miss Hannah, you're going to have to help me with this one." He grabbed the journals off the bed, praying that there was something in the second diary to make Shelby believe she was wanted and loved.

Rafe took the diaries home and stayed up all night, going through the second one. At times he'd felt sorry for Miss Hannah, and at other times he cursed her weakness. But the 1940s was a different era. Having a baby outside marriage wasn't acceptable behavior.

At six in the morning, while Rafe poured himself a fresh cup of coffee, Nonna Vittoria walked into the kitchen.

"*Buon giorno*, Rafaele," she said.

"Morning, Nonna." He leaned toward her for a kiss, taking for granted the simple show of affection. The kind of affection Shelby had never received growing up. He hugged Vittoria tightly.

"I love you, Nonna," he said, knowing he hadn't said it often enough.

"I love you, too." She smiled. "What brings this on?"

"Does something have to be the matter for me to tell you how I feel?"

Her wrinkled hands cupped his cheeks. "No, but your eyes tell me of your sadness. I know you are no longer a *bambino* but your nonna can still help you."

He took her hand and kissed it, savoring the sweetness of her gentle touch. "I'm in love with Shelby."

The older woman smiled and listened to her grandson's story about Shelby's life. The foster homes and the summer she had stayed at the cottage on the Stewart estate. Then the diaries and discovering that she was Hannah's granddaughter.

"She can't trust me enough to believe I won't leave her."

"I knew Shelby seemed familiar," Vittoria said. "She looks like Hannah." His grandmother's attention turned back to him. "We have to find a way to help her. She needs time to adjust to this discovery of who she is."

"I've tried, Nonna. She won't let me near her."

Nonna stood and kissed her grandson. "Listen to your heart, and you will find a way."

After Vittoria left, Rafe went back to the diary. He finished the part that revealed Shelby was Hannah's granddaughter. That page had been crumpled and stained with tears, and Rafe realized that Shelby must have quit reading here. She hadn't read on, because if she had, she would have known how much Miss Hannah wanted her.

July 4, 1976

There are fireworks going on at the park, and I can hear the children cheering. I wanted so badly to take my Shelby. I know she would love the pretty colors shooting off in the sky. In the time they stayed in the cottage, I came to love the child and want to be a part of her life. Maybe I can make up for the years I've lost with my own daughter.

July 10, 1979

The private investigator says he can't find any trace of Nola and Shelby. But I can't give up. I have a room all made up for little Shelby when they return. I know she likes pink—she told me so. I made her bedroom pink and bought her pink dresses for school. Just as soon as she comes back to me, everything will be fine. I'm going to take her to church and tell the world that she's my granddaughter. I promise I'll give her all the love I could never give her mother. Please come back to me, Shelby.

Rafe closed the diary. He didn't need to read any more to know how much Miss Hannah had loved her daughter and her granddaughter. If only he could get Shelby to read this. Then another thought came to him, and he knew what he had to do. He prayed his idea would keep Shelby here where she belonged.

A week later Shelby moved around the big house, doing her work, but even sitting at the computer reminded her of Rafe, of the hours she'd spent trying to teach him the program commands.

She tried refinishing the old dresser from the attic, but the enthusiasm she once had for Stewart Manor was no longer in her heart. She was numb. She'd managed to keep up with her graphic-arts business and even turned in an outline for her next Kellie Anne series, but nothing really seemed to matter anymore; she was just going through the motions. She'd been putting off contacting the Realtor, but by the end of the week, she was determined to make the call.

Friday morning there was a knock on the door, and Shelby went to answer it. She thought it would be the mailman, but instead, she was greeted by Bently Wolfe.

She opened the door. "Mr. Wolfe."

"Hello, Ms. Harris. I really hate to disturb you, since you work at home and all, but this is important."

Shelby stepped aside and allowed the distinguished, gray-haired gentleman in. "What can I do for you, Mr. Wolfe?"

"Well, as you know…" He paused and glanced around the entry, adorned with new textured wallpaper. An area rug she'd gotten at the estate sale covered the center of the room.

"Oh, you've done a wonderful job here." He went to the staircase and touched the newly polished wood. "This is exquisite. Rafe Covelli does excellent work."

Shelby nodded, feeling a lump rise in her throat. This was the most difficult part for her. This house had touches of Rafe everywhere. She would be reminded of him every day. How could she stay?

"He and his brother do wonderful work," Mr. Wolfe went on. "Have you seen any of the other homes they've restored?"

Shelby shook her head. She was ashamed for not going over to Jill's house when she'd been invited. But she'd always been leery of letting people get too close. Now she'd never get the chance to know if Jill could be her friend.

Mr. Wolfe walked back to her. "Well, the reason I've come is to tell you that this year Stewart Manor has been selected to receive the Haven Springs Historical Society plaque, confirming this house as a historical monument." He grinned. "We would be honored if you would act as the grand marshall of the eleventh annual Historical Festival of Homes."

Shelby's mouth dropped open. This was a real honor, but how could she? If anyone found out about her connection... "Thank you, Mr. Wolfe, but I really can't accept. I probably won't even be in town then. I'm selling Stewart Manor."

Mr. Wolfe didn't hide his shock. "Oh, I'm sorry to hear that," he said. "You've put so much work into this place. Anyone can see that you love it. I was also hoping you'd consider joining the historical society and helping with next year's festival. Rafe said you'd be perfect for the job, seeing as you have so many roots here."

Shelby gasped. "Rafe told you I had roots here?"

Mr. Wolfe raised a calming hand. "Don't worry, Shelby. May I call you Shelby?"

She nodded. "When Hannah Stewart was living, I was her lawyer. I knew all about her daughter—and granddaughter. I even helped her search for you after that summer you stayed here."

Shelby was having trouble understanding. "Her search?"

"At Hannah Stewart's request, I hired a private investigator to try to locate you. Your grandmother was going to attempt to get custody of you because of your mother's drug problem. But before we could find Nola, she overdosed on a mixture of alcohol and drugs."

"But I was in the foster-care system. She could have found me."

"After you left, Nola married and changed your name from Susan Shelby Brown to Susan Shelby Harris. We lost track of you." He took her hand. "I'm sorry, Shelby. We tried the best we could. I know your grandmother always thought she'd let you down by not finding you, but she really tried hard. I can only say she loved you very much."

Shelby was having trouble handling this new information. "You said Rafe told you who I was?"

Bently Wolfe nodded, looking worried. "He wasn't really breaking a confidence. Everyone knew I'd been Hannah's lawyer for years. He thought that I could explain things to you better than he could."

Her heart was in her throat. "Rafe sent you here?"

He nodded. "He said something about you being worried about disgracing the Stewart name." He reached for her hand and held it tight. "You aren't responsible for what your parents and grandparents did years ago. If anyone is innocent in this whole matter, it's you. Please, you have to believe that."

She finally smiled. "I think I do, Mr. Wolfe."

"Please call me Ben."

"Thank you, Ben, for being such a good friend to my grandmother." Shelby felt relief just saying the word. And thanks to Rafe, she could claim her family. *Rafe!* She had to see Rafe. "I want to thank you for stopping by, Ben. But I have to go see someone."

"I understand," he said. "But when you get some extra time, you'll need to come down to my office. There is the matter of a trust fund your grandmother set up for you."

"Trust fund? You don't mean...money?"

"Yes, I do." He grinned. "It should be enough to pay

off the mortgage, keep Stewart Manor and even add some nice pieces of furniture."

After he left, Shelby leaned against the closed door and drew a deep breath, then another. Rafe had done this for her. It hadn't mattered how much she pushed him away, he hadn't left her.

She rushed to the phone and dialed the construction office, but Angelina said she hadn't heard from Rafe all day and he wasn't answering his pager.

Disappointed, Shelby grabbed her purse and headed for her car. She was going to drive around town until she found Rafe. She had to tell him. To thank him.

She rushed out the back door and saw Ely working in the garden. She glanced up at the high summer sun. "Ely, don't you think that it's too hot for you to work out here?"

"I'm stopping in a few minutes. I only need to finish feeding the roses."

She walked between the bushes, catching the wonderful fragrance of the flowering pink roses. "They're so beautiful. You've done an incredible job restoring all this."

"I've enjoyed doing it. I haven't seen this garden looking this good since your grandmother—I mean Miss Hannah was here."

Shelby studied the old man. "You knew who I was, didn't you? You've known all along."

Ely nodded. "Yes, but it wasn't my place to tell you. I hoped Miss Hannah's diaries would explain everything."

"I guess I'm going to have to finish reading them."

"I believe Rafe returned them to the cottage."

"He did," she said, deciding she needed to read the diaries before she sought out Rafe.

Shelby waved goodbye to Ely and continued on toward the cottage. She stopped when the pristine white building came into view. The roof and broken windows had been replaced. The porch was brand-new, too. The rusty glider had been painted a bright spring green. Everything looked just like it had that summer twenty-three years ago.

Her hands shook as she opened the door and stepped inside. She gasped at the newly painted walls, the clean furniture. There was a vase of fresh-cut pink roses on the table. She heard a sound from the bedroom.

"Who's there?" she called.

Rafe stepped into view.

She gasped. After a week's absence, she was hungry for the sight of him. And what a sight. He was dressed in dark slacks and a wine-colored sport shirt, and the late-afternoon light spilling in from the window behind him made him an imposing figure. But that didn't stop her arms aching with the need to wrap herself around him. He could set her blood racing with one look.

"The cottage looks wonderful," she murmured.

"I wanted to bring the place back to what it was like at a happy time in your life. Ely told me exactly how it looked."

They both stood there for a long moment, Shelby's heart drumming in her chest as she wondered what to do next. Rafe seemed to be waiting for her to make the first move.

"What took you so long to get here?" he finally asked. "Were you still trying to decide if we should be together?"

"Why do you keep rescuing me?"

He shook his head. "You're wrong, *cara*. You're the one who's rescued *me*. From the first time you flashed your smile, you made me feel alive. When you kissed me, I'd never tasted anything so sweet, so tender. I never knew how lonely I'd been until you unlocked my heart and stole my soul and made me fall in love. You are the other part of me, Shelby. I don't think I can live without you."

Shelby closed the gap between them and put her arms

around him. She wiped the tears from her face against his shirt and heard his breathing crack.

"If it's not too late, will you take me back?" she asked timidly.

Rafe shook with need. He still didn't have everything he wanted from Shelby. "Why do you want to come back to me, Shelby?"

She looked up at him with those incredible green eyes. "Oh, Rafe...I love you."

"But there's more, Shelby. You have to trust me enough to believe I love you more than anything and that I will always be there for you."

"I do. I realized today I've always trusted you. I've shared more with you than I have with anyone ever." Her eyes, wet with tears, met his. "I told things I never told anyone. I want to share more. I want to share everything with you. My life and my—"

Before she could finish, his mouth captured hers. An urgent hunger burst within her, filling one hollow ache while creating another need. She moved against him, feeling his need for her.

Finally he released her and smiled. "Why, Ms. Shelby, are you asking me to marry you?"

Her finger toyed with his lower lip. "Unlike my grandmother and my mother, I'm going to hang on to my man, no matter what it takes."

"Now I like that idea. Just plan on a wedding soon."

Her hand slid across his chest. She loved the feel of the muscles under his shirt. "But we still have a lot of work to do on the house. I'd like to have a garden wedding."

He groaned deep in his throat. "Okay, I'll finish Stewart Manor. Fast!"

She pursed her lips as if trying to decide something.

"What do you think about turning the attic into my office? A place where I can work on my writing."

He gasped as she unbuttoned his shirt and her lips made contact with his skin. "Green eyes, I'll build you whatever it takes to make you my bride." He grew serious. "I love you."

"Oh, Rafe, I love you, too."

His mouth came down on hers in another searing kiss, letting her know that any future deals with her would come with an extended contract, one that lasted a lifetime.

Epilogue

Frances Newcomb on the Town

The Covelli-Stewart wedding took place on the twenty-eighth of September, at Stewart Manor, in Miss Hannah's rose garden. The bride arrived in a horse-drawn carriage lent to her by the Haven Springs Historical Society. Ms. Shelby Harris-Stewart was dressed in a fitted gown of antique lace with a long flowing train. Her hair was adorned with pink and white rosebuds, which also made up her bridal bouquet. As she stepped out of the carriage, Ely Cullen escorted her from the circular drive to the rose garden, where she followed her attendants, Jill Covelli and Angelina Covelli, down the aisle dusted with rose petals, where friends, family and well-wishers awaited.

Ms. Shelby was met by her groom, Rafaele Covelli, Jr., under the rose arbor. He looked handsome and directed an adoring look at his lovely bride. By the time the vows were exchanged, there wasn't a dry eye in the house. The handsome couple kissed, then invited everyone into Stewart Manor for the reception.

This wedding was definitely the Haven Springs social event of the year.

Smiling, Shelby climbed out of the four-poster bed, careful not to disturb the breakfast tray Rafe had brought up for her earlier in honor of their two-week anniversary. But when Shelby had kissed her husband to thank him, the lovely breakfast had been forgotten and they'd ended up making love.

Dressed in her satin, mint-green nightgown, Shelby walked across the rose-colored carpet into the suite's bathroom. Rafe was standing at the sink shaving, a towel draped around his waist.

Shelby blushed, remembering the past two weeks of their marriage and how tender and loving her husband had been. How much they'd shared with each other the week they'd spent at Jill and Rick's lake cottage. A longer honeymoon was planned as soon as Stewart Manor was completed and Covelli and Sons' contract with Delany Construction was under way. But they didn't really need to go away. Rafe gave her all the attention she needed here.

"Rafe, the newspaper says our wedding was the social event of the year."

He frowned and stopped shaving. "And that doesn't make you happy?"

"Well, what about Jill and Rick's wedding? Won't they be hurt to know their wedding wasn't the social event of the year?"

Rafe raised his chin and glided the razor along his neck, then rinsed the blade in the sinkful of water. He turned to her and smiled. "Honey, I hate to disappoint you, but Frances Newcomb has been the society editor for over thirty years, and she always writes that every wedding in Haven Springs is the social event of the year.''

"Oh, isn't that nice. She does it for everyone.'' Shelby leaned against the doorjamb and smiled.

Rafe stole another glance at his bride. She looked too tempting standing there in her nightgown. And damn, here he had a meeting scheduled this morning to go over the plans for the new housing tract. Still he couldn't help but ask, "Something else I can do for you, Mrs. Covelli?"

Her green eyes lit up and a jolt of awareness hit him right in the gut.

"My, aren't you energetic this morning, Mr. Covelli.''

He wiped his face with the towel and went to her. "You're the cause of that. Have I told you how much I love you?''

"I love you, too. So much it scares me sometimes,'' she confessed.

"Don't be afraid, Shelby. I'm here for you. And I plan to be for a very long time.'' He knew the best way to convince her was to show her. He leaned toward her and covered her mouth with a kiss. It started slow and easy, but quickly became hot and searing. But that was how their loving had been from the beginning. He angled his head to deepen the kiss, and his tongue pushed inside to taste her hunger, too. She didn't disappoint him as she moved into his embrace, combed her fingers into his hair, pulling him closer.

Rafe slipped the straps of her gown down her arms, exposing her lovely breasts, then with another tug, the satin fell to the floor. With a heated look in her green eyes, one he'd come to know well the past two weeks, she reached out and pulled at the towel at his waist. It, too, found its way to the floor.

Rafe groaned. "You know I have a meeting this morning, *cara.*"

"And I'm supposed to be at Jill's in an hour. We're going furniture shopping." She stepped closer, her finger tracing the hair on his chest. He sucked in a breath and she glanced down to see the proud evidence of her action. "How about I make you a deal, Mr. Covelli?"

He grinned. This game was getting interesting. "Let's hear it."

"How about Rick and Tony sit in on the meeting for you, and I call Jill and tell her I'll be a little late?"

They both made the calls and then Rafe swung her up in his arms and carried her back to the bed. Then he lay down beside her. "I don't think we're fooling anyone." He kissed her, then pulled back. "Shelby, you know you don't have to make deals with me so I'll make love to you. I have trouble keeping my hands off you."

She glanced away. "Oh, Rafe, I've never been this happy in my entire life. Sometimes I get afraid it's all going to disappear."

He made her look at him. "I'm never going away, *cara*. I fought too hard—my family curse, an old diary and one stubborn woman. If you think I'm going anywhere, I guess I'm just going to have to keep you here until I can convince you otherwise."

He relaxed when he saw she was fighting a smile. "It won't be easy."

"Oh, I think I can handle the job. I just hope you aren't too upset you're not turning this place into a bed-and-breakfast. I know how much you wanted—"

Shelby sealed Rafe's lips with a finger. A thrill rushed through her as she realized how lucky she was to have this man in her life. "I only wanted to fill this house with people. But you're all the people I need. You're my family."

"Speaking of family, I have something for you." He rolled away, opened the drawer on the nightstand and pulled out a box. "I meant to give you this last night as an anniversary gift, but you distracted me."

Shelby lifted the lid and parted the tissue. Inside was a picture of a young woman. Her hairstyle and dress were of a different era. "Oh, Rafe, it's my grandmother." The picture beneath it was of a man in an army uniform. "And my grandfather?"

Rafe nodded. "I wanted you to be able to have some family pictures for the mantel downstairs." He set the photos aside and reclined with her on the bed. "And, of course, if you're willing we can add some of our own."

"Why, Mr. Covelli, are you offering me a deal?" she asked teasingly, loving this man more every day. Having his children would be a dream come true.

He nodded. "Give me a little time and maybe I can convince you." His mouth met hers, sealing the deal for their lifetime together. Through the rough times and the good times, Shelby knew he would always be there, never letting her feel lonely again. She finally realized it wasn't the structure that made a home. It was Rafe and his love.

And she was finally home...for good.

*   *   *   *   *

*Don't miss Angelina's story
when Patricia Thayer's miniseries*
WITH THESE RINGS
continues with
THE MAN, THE RING, THE WEDDING
*available December 1999
only from Silhouette Romance.*

Silhouette ROMANCE™

VIRGIN BRIDES

**Your favorite authors
tell more heartwarming
stories of lovely brides
who discover love...
for the first time....**

July 1999 GLASS SLIPPER BRIDE
Arlene James (SR #1379)
Bodyguard Jack Keller had to protect innocent
Jillian Waltham—day and night. But when his assignment
became a matter of temporary marriage, would Jack's hardened
heart need protection...from Jillian, his glass slipper bride?

September 1999 MARRIED TO THE SHEIK
Carol Grace (SR #1391)
Assistant Emily Claybourne secretly loved her boss, and now Sheik
Ben Ali had finally asked her to marry him! But Ben was only
interested in a temporary union...until Emily started showing him
the joys of marriage—and love....

November 1999 THE PRINCESS AND THE COWBOY
Martha Shields (SR #1403)
When runaway Princess Josephene Francoeur needed a
short-term husband, cowboy Buck Buchanan was the perfect
choice. But to wed him, Josephene had to tell a *few* white lies,
which worked...until "Josie Freeheart" realized she wanted
to love her rugged cowboy groom forever!

Available at your favorite retail outlet.

SILHOUETTE BOOKS
is proud to announce the arrival of

THE BABY OF THE MONTH CLUB:

the latest installment of author
Marie Ferrarella's
popular miniseries.

When pregnant Juliette St. Claire met Gabriel Saldana than she discovered he wasn't the struggling artist he claimed to be. An undercover agent, Gabriel had been sent to Juliette's gallery to nab his prime suspect: Juliette herself. But when he discovered her innocence, would he win back Juliette's heart and convince her that he was the daddy her baby needed?

Don't miss Juliette's induction into
THE BABY OF THE MONTH CLUB
in September 1999.
Available at your favorite retail outlet.

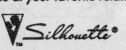

Of all the unforgettable families created by
#1 *New York Times* bestselling author

NORA ROBERTS

the Donovans are the most extraordinary. For, along with
their irresistible appeal, they've inherited some rather
remarkable gifts from their Celtic ancestors.

Coming in November 1999

THE DONOVAN LEGACY

3 full-length novels in one special volume:

CAPTIVATED: Hardheaded skeptic Nash Kirkland has *always*
kept his feelings in check, until he falls under the bewitching
spell of mysterious Morgana Donovan.

ENTRANCED: Desperate to find a missing child, detective
Mary Ellen Sutherland dubiously enlists beguiling
Sebastian Donovan's aid and discovers his uncommon abilities
include a talent for seduction.

CHARMED: Enigmatic healer Anastasia Donovan would do
anything to save the life of handsome Boone Sawyer's
daughter, even if it means revealing her secret to the man
who'd stolen her heart.

Also in November 1999 from Silhouette Intimate Moments

ENCHANTED

Lovely, guileless Rowan Murray is drawn to darkly enigmatic
Liam Donovan with a power she's never imagined possible. But
before Liam can give Rowan his love, he must first reveal to
her his incredible secret.

V *Silhouette* ®

Available at your favorite retail outlet.